"YOU DON'T KNOW WHO THE HELL YOU'RE DEALING WITH—WE'RE THE YODERS!"

Fred stopped in front of her and raised the barrel of the Winchester until it was inches away from Jessie's chest. "Take your jacket off," he ordered.

"You're making a real mistake, Fred. Why don't you and your brother put those guns away and let us ride off your land without any trouble."

"Sometimes we like trouble, pretty woman. So do as I say."

Jessie removed her jacket. Her heart began to thump faster. Out of the corner of her eye, she saw the samurai reach into his vest pocket, but Arnie was so intent on seeing her expose her breasts that he wasn't even watching Ki.

"Now, unbutton your shirt and open it wide."

Jessie shook her head. "No."

Fred reached out to her. That was the moment Jessie had been waiting for. She brought her knee up hard between his legs. Ki's hand shot forward and the *shuriken* blade whistled through the air. It struck Arnie in the shoulder and the rifle in his hands exploded . . .

◆→ WESLEY ELLIS ◆→

LONE STAR

AND THE
NEVADA BLOODBATH

J

JOVE BOOKS, NEW YORK

LONE STAR AND THE NEVADA BLOODBATH

A Jove book/published by arrangement with
the author

PRINTING HISTORY
Jove edition/September 1988

ISBN: 0-515-09708-X

Jove books are published by The Berkley Publishing Group,
200 Madison Avenue, New York, New York 10016.
The name "JOVE" and the "J" logo
are trademarks belonging to Jove Publications, Inc.

PRINTED IN THE UNITED STATES OF AMERICA

10 9 8 7 6 5 4 3 2 1

Chapter 1

Jessie Starbuck could feel the perspiration trickling down her backbone. The wood-smoke from the laboring Virginia and Truckee Railroad engine made her slightly nauseated, but what a panoramic view of western Nevada lay stretched out before her! Jessie and her samurai companion, Ki, had boarded the train at Roundhouse Station in Carson City less than an hour earlier. The V and T Railroad, its boiler dripping and steaming, had given two blasts on its steam whistle and headed directly eastward into the high desert sage. Off to her right she now caught glimpses of the sun as it sparkled off the Carson River. A line of cottonwood trees led her eye farther out into the desert. But for some inexplicable reason, the huge lumberyards and numerous sawmills all sat abandoned.

Jessica's lovely sea-green eyes studied the tin rooftops of the sawmills and the smokeless stacks jutting up against the pale, sun-blasted hills. She had come to investigate the Comstock Lode and perhaps buy herself a silver and gold mine. But the absence of activity along the Carson River told her that something was amiss.

"Ki, it seems to me that if the mines on the Comstock Lode are doing as well as I am supposed to believe, every sawmill on the Carson River would be filled with new logs for underground shoring."

1

The tall, slender Eurasian beside her nodded but said nothing, for he was not a man who made idle talk. To the samurai's way of thinking, Jessie, as always, was very observant and her reasoning quite flawless. She would, of course, ask that exact question of the men who awaited them in Virginia City. It was precisely the kind of question that would demonstrate to any astute businessman that Jessica Starbuck was a woman who missed little.

For her own part, Jessie had not expected an answer from her protector and faithful companion. Ki was a samurai, a martial-arts master, whose actions spoke far more eloquently than his words. His very presence was a comfort to her and, now as always when they traveled together, she was aware that they made quite a pair. Jessie Starbuck was, by any definition, stunningly beautiful, with her blond hair and hourglass figure. She had long, shapely legs and a narrow waist accentuated by the fullness of her bosom. Because of the flying cinders and the thick smoke from the steam engine, Jessie wore a dark duster over her dress, but would have felt much more comfortable in Levis and a blouse, the day-to-day working clothes that she habitually wore on her huge Circle Star Ranch down in Texas.

"Miss Starbuck." A voice behind her spoke up. Its owner introduced himself. "My name is Ethan Dorr and I could not help but overhear your question just now. May I comment, please?"

Jessie regarded a middle-aged, rather scholarly looking man with a receding hairline, baggy jowls and watery eyes that blinked myopically behind thick bifocals. The man was wearing a heavy tweed suit and tie, and he was much too warm. His chubby red face was bathed in sweat.

"Of course, Mr. Dorr."

"Thank you!" he said with gratitude. "You see, I am a mining engineer from San Francisco. I've been called over

2

here to visit the Comstock to ask precisely the questions you have just raised. The very fact of the matter is that there is a supreme shortage of good timber for underground shoring. That's causing a great many cave-ins, I'm sorry to say. It's my understanding that men are buried underground almost daily."

"Why, that's horrible!"

"Of course it is. But there seems to be little by way of an immediate solution, Miss Starbuck. As you saw in Carson City, the eastern slope of the Sierra Nevadas has been logged almost clean. What timber there remains is runty and of poor quality, and yet it continues to be logged. Poor-quality timber such as that could not possibly withstand the tremendous underground weight it is often forced to suspend. Not possibly!"

The intense little man shook his head vigorously. He appeared to Jessie to be extremely excitable and quite upset. "Go on," Jessie told him.

"I'm saying that the only premium-grade timber left within fifty miles of the Comstock Lode is to be found at Lake Tahoe on the California–Nevada boundary line!"

Jessie frowned. It did not seem possible. Yet she recalled that early this morning when she and Ki had taken a walk around Carson City, they had both remarked at how the eastern slope of the Sierras had been stripped of much of its timber and that the hills they were now approaching had been completely denuded of piñon and juniper pine. "What about those cottonwood trees?" she asked, pointing out the window toward the Carson River. "Some of them look very large and strong."

The little engineer almost laughed. "My dear woman, cottonwood is terribly weak and subject to stress failure under pressure. Besides, that little bit of timber would not last a single mine even one month, and there are dozens of

3

big mining operations in existence on the Comstock. Add those to the thousands of little claims staked by pathetic prospectors from one end of Six Mile Canyon to the other, and you can well see why millions of board feet of prime lumber have already either been burned by the steam engines that power the stamping and sawmills, or else used in shoring or for heating fuel."

"Yes," Jessie said as the V and T Railroad began to climb a series of switchbacks that would take it into Virginia City. She studied the rocky, treeless hillsides with a sense of awe and respect. This was hard country. The air was thin, and she knew the summers would be blistering and the winters terribly cold. The luckier prospectors around here lived in little shacks, but most survived the elements by sleeping in tiny caves hacked out of the mountainside, or even in little holes in the earth covered by paper, brush, or pieces of discarded tin. Jessie felt sorry for men who had to live like rodents and suffer such hardship. The entire scene was shocking, and she had never seen so much activity confined to such a small area of canyon. Everywhere she looked she saw rough-looking miners digging away at the hillsides. Their tailings were like large mole hills numbering in the thousands.

"They'll never strike it rich," the mining engineer said with a sad shake of his head. "The silver and gold found here is entirely different than that which started the Forty-Niner gold rush."

Jessie knew very little about gold. Her father had built a huge shipping and export business that had made him a fortune. When Alex Starbuck had been murdered by a vicious international cartel, Jessie had been his only heir. She had inherited his many holdings and his money, but she mostly thought of herself as a cattlewoman. But cattle prices had been down for several years, and Jessie remem-

4

bered her father had told her that diversification was the key to a continuing strong rate of growth for the Starbuck empire. Jessie had taken that advice seriously. She had further expanded her late father's vast industrial holdings in Europe as well as his coffee and sugar plantations in South America. She had recently been to South Africa to buy a diamond mine, but this grim Comstock Lode was quite another matter entirely. And though free information, like free advice, was usually worthless, Jessie thought that it would not hurt at all to listen to this man and learn something.

"How is this so different from the Forty-Niner gold rush?" she asked.

Dorr seemed very pleased to have the chance to educate her and the samurai. "Well, the California gold rush revolved entirely around—at least in its early stages before they turned to hydraulics—placer mining. That means that the gold was easy to find because it was on the surface. It could be found in rivers, or under rocks. There were rich deposits right on the surface. But here in Nevada, the gold and silver is much too deep under the ground for those poor fellows with their picks and shovels to even hope to reach. It's a pity; and though they would never listen to me, I could save them all a great deal of heart- and back-ache if they would only understand that the Comstock gold is deposited in pockets hundreds of feet below the surface. This is hard and deep rock mining, Miss Starbuck. It is terribly dangerous and requires the finest miners that can be found anywhere in the world. For that reason, it also offers the highest wages, five dollars a day for an eight-hour shift, and the mines never shut down. The steam engines run continuously and so do the pumps, which can only attempt to keep the mines dry."

Jessie nodded. She was not completely ignorant of the

5

Comstock. "What I am told is that it takes huge amounts of capital to have any chance of success here."

"Oh, my yes!" Dorr said, his little eyes dancing. "Look at the big mines and you will readily see that there are tens of thousands of dollars invested in big steam engines and underground mining machinery. The men in, say the famous Ophir Mine, all go down in steel and wire cages. These cages are lowered as much as a thousand feet underground. Sun Mountain, which is where Virginia City is, can only be described as being riddled with tunnels. Miles and miles of them."

"Have you heard of the Lucky Lady Mine?" Jessie asked, because Wild Bill Evans, an old friend of hers, had given her a tip that this particular mine might be bought at a reasonable price, and that it had a great deal of potential because of its excellent location.

"No." Dorr frowned. "How many men does it employ, and what is its weekly tonnage?"

"I have no idea."

The mining engineer shook his head as if dismissing the Lucky Lady as being of no importance whatsoever. "Believe me, Miss Starbuck. More money is probably made on the Comstock by selling worthless stock in mining companies than is made from the ore itself. Why, over in San Francisco, thousands of wealthy men who should have known far better than to invest in things they know nothing about have seen their fortunes swallowed up and lost."

"That may be true," Jessie said, "but there are always men—and women—who profit and who invest wisely. My advisers have told me that the Comstock will last for many years, perhaps even decades."

"It may well do that," Dorr admitted. "By my calculations, there is another ten million's worth of gold and silver under Sun Mountain. But the problem is that all the time it gets harder and more expensive to reach. If gold is selling for eight dollars an ounce and it costs ten to bring it up and smelt it down, what good is it?"

"None," Jessie said. "None at all unless the factors of production drop."

Dorr removed his glasses and polished the ash from their lenses. "'Factors of production,'" he mused. "Isn't that a term coined by a French economist?"

"German," Jessie said.

"Exactly what does it mean?"

"It means the costs of doing business. Wages, supplies, interest on investment, capital expenditures—"

The mining engineer interrupted her in his excitement. "And underground shoring for the mines that has become prohibitively expensive." He sighed. "I'm here to try and figure out some solution to the problem. But there really is none. You can't substitute anything for cheap timbering."

Jessie pursed her lips. "Then in that case, the mine operators and investors had better build a railroad up to Lake Tahoe and try to lower the cost of their future lumber."

"It isn't quite that simple."

Jessie listened as the V and T engineer began to blast his whistle. The train entered a tunnel and, for a moment, the bright light of day was transformed into inky darkness. The smoke, without anywhere to go, blew off the ceiling of the tunnel and back into the passenger cars, almost asphyxiating the occupants. When the train finally emerged in sunlight again, they were all choking and coughing. The mining engineer seemed to be completely overcome. He was lying slumped across his seat behind Jessie.

Ki saw him too, and they both reached for the man, thinking that he might have suffered a heart attack or apoplexy. But they were wrong.

"He's been stabbed to death," Ki said, pulling the man's

tweed jacket aside to reveal the handle of a knife protruding from just under Dorr's rib cage.

Jessie glanced quickly around the passenger car. It was loaded with rough miners and unsavory-looking men of all descriptions. "There is no way in the world to tell who did this, is there?"

Ki shook his head. His black eyes surveyed each man. No one was paying them the slightest attention. They looked tired or bored, and many of them were still coughing and choking. "The only question that we can even attempt to answer is, why was he killed?" Ki propped the dead engineer's bowler over his face so that he looked as if he was sleeping. There was nothing to be gained by causing a stir.

Jessie considered the question, but drew a complete blank. "I have no idea. Perhaps he had enemies he'd made from previous trips to the Comstock."

"Yes," Ki said, "that is quite possible. But there is an even greater possibility."

"And that is?"

"That is that Mr. Dorr was killed because he was telling you things that someone in this coach did not want revealed."

Jessie blinked. "But what . . ."

The samurai shrugged. "I don't know. He told you nothing that wouldn't seem to be common knowledge. But he might have said more before we arrived in Virginia City."

Jessie nodded in understanding and took a seat beside the dead engineer, hoping that she had in no way contributed to his murder.

She stared out across a hundred miles of desert wasteland that stretched all the way to Utah Territory. A feeling

8

of foreboding assailed her spirits, and she retraced every word of the conversation, but without results.

Mr. Dorr had been murdered. Jessie kept telling herself that she had nothing whatsoever to do with it, but something inside of her knew better.

Chapter 2

Mr. Andre La Fleur was waiting at the Virginia City train station. He was not alone. Beside him stood three more gentlemen in equally stiff white collars and expensive black suits. Jessie saw them through the window of the passenger car, and she frowned. "It looks like we've got the welcoming committee out in full force."

Ki glanced at the assembly of bankers and stockbrokers. "Yes," he said, "that's a sign that they're overeager. Beware, Jessie. They have a lean and hungry look in their eyes."

She nodded. "Before we talk business, I want to get poor Mr. Dorr off this train and to a funeral home. We'll also want to pay a visit to the sheriff and see if he can shed some light on this."

"I don't think Mr. La Fleur will be too pleased about that. He appears to be a little uncomfortable."

It was true. The four men were standing right in the path of the steam that rushed out of the brakes, and were nearly being blasted off the platform. Jessie could see La Fleur's mouth, twisted into a grimace of outrage as the offended man waved his fist up at the locomotive engineer.

La Fleur was ignored, his shout of anger completely muted by the steam engine. The train ground to a screeching halt and the engineer blasted his whistle for everyone to depart. No one needed urging. The passengers, covered with soot, their eyes bloodshot from the cinders and smoke, were all too eager to get off and distance themselves from the besotted train. Jessie was content to wait until the aisle was clear. Virginia City itself was enough to absorb her attention for quite some time.

The city was perched on the side of Sun Mountain, and every street was a good fifty feet higher or lower than the next. Freight and huge ore wagons jammed the thoroughfares as teamsters whipped their straining animals up and down the steep mountainside. St. Mary of the Mountains Catholic Church, with its brick walls and its towering white steeple, was an easy landmark, but there were plenty of other buildings equally as impressive, such as the Fourth Ward School, and the huge mining works with their towering smokestacks and hoisting scaffolding. Virginia City was a bustling city of nearly twenty thousand hearty souls who had come from around the world to earn high wages or even a chance of striking it rich.

"Imagine," Jessie said as she shook her head, "how shocked the Californians from the lush Sierra Nevadas with their turbulent, beautiful rivers must have been when they first saw this harsh desert country."

"They came for the gold," Ki said. "When men seek fortune, they see nothing except the dirt under their feet."

"I suppose that's true," Jessie replied, "but still, it must have been quite an adjustment. Look at the cemeteries. They're already full."

It was true. There was a big Catholic cemetery and a Protestant one as well, and though the Comstock Lode had been in existence only a few years before the Civil War, both cemeteries were already spilling over their fenced boundaries. Beyond them, a sea of rolling brown hills and small mountain ranges seemed to reach forever.

12

Jessie saw La Fleur, already grown impatient, pushing his way through the throng of departing passengers to come aboard. His rushed manner irritated Jessie, though she could not exactly say why. Maybe it was because someone had just been murdered; because she might in some way be partially responsible she did not wish to discuss business this day. Also, it was her opinion that sometimes a person needed a few days to acclimate herself to new and unfamiliar surroundings before making a major investment decision.

"Miss Starbuck, I presume?" he asked with a wide smile that revealed perfect and unusually white teeth.

Jessie looked up to regard the swarthy, undeniably handsome man. He was in his mid-thirties and quite debonaire. He had black hair and a twinkle in his eye that went right along with the exaggerated flair of the tips of his waxed mustache. He bowed like a European, with one hand across the front of his flat belly and the other pressed to the small of his back.

"I am," Jessie said, rising to her feet.

He straightened and looked boldly into her eyes. "I am Mr. Andre La Fleur and I sincerely apologize for the heat and the soot, Miss Starbuck. I would have preferred that you had accepted our offer to send a special coach down to Carson City to transport you and your servant up to our city."

Jessie's eyes sparked. "Ki is *not* my servant. He is my friend."

The banker managed a weak grin and he glanced at Ki but did not really bother to see him. "I'm so sorry. Of course he is! A Chinaman can be—"

Now it was Ki's turn to bristle at the insult. "I haven't a drop of Chinese blood in my body," he snapped. "My fa-

13

ther was an American. My mother was of royal Nipponese blood."

La Fleur finally seemed to realize that he had already committed an inexcusable faux pas. "A thousand pardons, sir!" he cried, bowing to Ki at the waist and extending his hand as he would to an equal. "But of course we are as honored to greet you as we are Miss Starbuck, Mr . . . Ki?"

"Just Ki," the samurai said in a brusque tone of voice.

"Of course. Please, I have some gentlemen waiting outside who are very eager to see you. We have a luncheon planned at the finest restaurant on the Comstock. I hope you like roast chicken with—"

Jessie shook her head so emphatically that the man's voice trailed away to nothing. She added, "Mr. La Fleur, if you'll look over the back of the seat next to us you will see a man."

La Fleur shrugged. "I miss nothing. I see his feet and know he is either asleep or drunk. It is shameful, I agree, but . . ."

"You miss the fact that he has just been murdered," Jessie said, almost glad to puncture the man's totally supercilious demeanor.

The effect of her words could hardly have been more pronounced. La Fleur's square jaw dropped and, quite unconscious of himself, he jumped back half a step. "Murdered?"

"Yes, in that long tunnel a few miles down the mountain."

La Fleur took a mechanical step forward and peered over the seat at the dead mining engineer. "My God!" he whispered, his complexion beginning to pale. "He *is* dead. And right here next to you! How . . . how perfectly revolting. I promise you I will speak to the management of the V and T Railroad at once! This kind of thing cannot be permitted to take place in the presence of ladies and gentle-men."

Jessie glanced at Ki, who rolled his eyes in absolute disbelief. La Fleur, for all his fancy manners and expensive tailoring, was one of the most pompous and callous men either Jessie or Ki had ever met.

"Why don't you find a porter and then let's allow them to send for a hearse and a mortician?" Ki suggested.

"Yes," the banker said. "Yes, that is an excellent idea! There are a number of morticians in Virginia City. Excellent, every . . . Do you know who he was?"

"His name was Dorr. He was a mining engineer."

"Oh, yes!" the banker exclaimed, finally getting a grip on himself. "I know of the man. He was said to be brilliant but too outspoken, and his methods were inclined to be radical."

"Well," Jessie said, "whatever his opinions, they are lost forever. We would like to speak with the sheriff of Virginia City. A homicide report is no doubt needed and there will be questions."

"Please, allow me to spare you such unpleasantness," the banker begged. "I can find someone else who can take your story and then provide the details."

"No," Jessie said. "We will remain here until the morti-cian and the sheriff have arrived. I'm afraid the luncheon you had planned will have to be postponed for a few days."

"But . . . Miss Starbuck! Like yourself, I am devastated by this terrible act of violence, yet it must not be allowed to interfere with our plans. You've come a great distance to see the mine we believe will enhance your already sizable fortune. The mine is for sale and we are receiving other very attractive offers. Surely you understand why; even a single day's delay is very costly."

Jessie heard an alarm bell of warning go off in her

brain. She remembered that her father, Alex Starbuck, had always subscribed to a tested business axiom that worked. He believed that the more anxious a seller is to part with property, the less anxious ought to be the buyer. The converse was equally true. Andre La Fleur was very eager to sell and that made Jessie all the more determined to forestall a quick decision.

"Please send for the mortician and the sheriff," she reiterated. "We will remain here with the body and then we will take our leave."

"Very well. But I have rooms for you at the Regency Hotel," La Fleur said, his body revealing that he had accepted this small delay and considered it a defeat. "They are the best."

Jessie preferred the banker when he was depressed. "Thank you. You may call tomorrow morning at ten when we can discuss your business proposition. Please bring the earnings reports and the investment records. I want all the assay reports, the depreciation schedules, and of course any geological studies as to the value of the property. What did you call your mine?"

"The Montezuma," La Fleur said, trying to flog his own enthusiasm. "We can prove to you that the yield during the past three years has exceeded—"

"Tomorrow," Jessie said with mounting impatience. "Please explain to your friends our change of plans and express our apologies."

La Fleur was persistent, but he wasn't obtuse. He realized that he had been summarily dismissed and he had no choice but to accept the fact with as much grace and dignity as possible. Expanding his chest and raising his chin, he said, "Of course, Miss Starbuck. Tomorrow at ten."

He turned to Ki. "Mr. Ki, it has been my pleasure."

But La Fleur didn't look pleased at all. There was some-

16

thing in his eyes that mocked his words and made it clearer than day that he did not appreciate having to shake the hands of an Oriental, even a half-Oriental.

Ki understood that look very well. He was dressed in his usual dark jeans, uncollared shirt, and leather vest which contained his *shuriken,* or star-blade weapons. On his feet he wore rope-and-cotton sandals rather than the typical western boots favored by most men. His hair was long and he wore a braided leather headband to keep it from his eyes. The samurai was an oddity, and this created a barrier between himself and men who measured other men purely in terms of the level of their conformity. They did not understand him or his background or what he was doing traveling with a beautiful Caucasian woman. Ki's very *karma* was completely alien to them, and what men like La Fleur did not understand, they instinctively distrusted.

Ki understood. It did not matter. He had sworn to devote his life to being the protector of Alex Starbuck's beautiful daughter. Like all samurai, Ki needed a mission and a reason for his special talents. He was an expert in the ancient and venerated art of *te,* or open-hand fighting, and devoted himself to the daily ritual of keeping his skills honed and always being prepared for anything that might threaten Jessie.

"I guess we just wait right here," Jessie said, taking her seat again. "I would say that the sheriff would be along within a quarter-hour."

"The mortician will arrive first," Ki said with assurance.

"How do you know that?"

"Because he is the one who stands to profit the most."

Jessie nodded. That was very logical reasoning and deduction. That was also very much like the samurai. Ki was the most logical man in the world, and that meant that he

17

was usually correct. "I just hope that the sheriff might be able to give us some idea why this man was killed," she said.

"He won't," the samurai said.

Jessie frowned and looked at Ki, thinking how his unwavering self-assurance could at times be very irritating. "How do you know that?"

"Because he would not profit from knowing such a man."

Jessie shook her head in disbelief. "Sometimes you are the most vexing man I have ever known, Ki!"

"I know," he told her with a straight face, though it took great control to hide his grin.

Jessie ground her teeth together and leaned her head back against the seat. The sun seemed to beat with increasing passion down on the rooftop of their passenger car. Because the car was stationary there was no longer any breeze from movement, though at least the soot wasn't drifting back from the locomotive and there were no more sparks flying in the windows.

Jessie thought about Mr. Dorr and wondered why La Fleur and his matched penguins were so damned eager to sell the Montezuma Mine. It was too bad that Mr. Dorr wasn't still alive. Maybe he could have told her.

The sheriff's name was Cap Slater. He was a quiet, thoughtful and competent looking man, nearing an age to be thinking about retirement. Jessie related the death of the mining engineer and he heard her out before he even ventured a comment.

"My guess is that it was a pure case of robbery. You could tell by the clothes the man wore that he would have a pretty big wad of money on him."

"But . . ."

18

"Did anyone see if his wallet was still on his body?" the sheriff asked, even as the mining engineer was being taken away.

"I did," Ki said. "It was missing. So was his gold watch, Jessie."

She somehow felt a little betrayed. "Why didn't you tell me?"

Ki looked ashamed of himself. "I would have. At any rate, I still don't believe the motive was robbery. If that were the case, they would have tried to rob you, not Mr. Dorr."

"That's right, Sheriff," Jessie said. "How do you account for that?"

"That's easy," the lawman replied. "Some men would be squeamish over killing a woman. Some men would take a look at your martial-arts friend here and just know that he was big trouble."

Ki nodded. This sheriff missed very little.

Slater continued, "I'll need you to come up to my office and fill out a report on the murder. It'll only take a minute, but it's required by the county coroner's office. Damned paperwork they come up with these days is enough to drive a good lawman into another line altogether."

The sheriff had a buggy and they rode up the street with him. His office was neat and had the look of a professional. Without wasting time in small talk, he had both Jessie and Ki fill out reports on the murder, and as soon as that was finished he said, "Is there anything else you can tell me? Did you see any of the other passengers with blood on their hands or clothing? Anything at all?"

Both Ki and Jessie shook their heads. Jessie said, "I imagine you've been through that V and T Railroad tunnel all too many times yourself. As you know, the blackness is absolute and the duration at least three minutes. Whoever did it probably had left the coach before we emerged from the tunnel."

The sheriff nodded. "Yeah, I suspect so. Do you still think that robbery was a secondary motive?"

"Yes," both Ki and Jessie said together.

Jessie explained. "Mr. Dorr was very outspoken in his opinion that the Comstock is doomed without proper timbering—timbering that he claimed can be found in sufficient quantities only up at Lake Tahoe. Is that true?"

The sheriff threw up his hands. "That's not for me to say. I just try and keep a lid on this town, not figure out what's going on underground. Course, like everyone else, I'm heavily invested in mining stocks. And if that market were to crash, a lot of us who got in early and figure we have a pretty nice nest egg for retirement would suddenly find that we're wiped out. So sure, I'd like to tell you that there is nothing to that rumor. Only I'm afraid there is. We're losing miners every day to cave-ins. I would rather face John Wesley Hardin in a stand-up gunfight than make my living under Sun Mountain."

Jessie appreciated the lawman's candor. "Have you ever heard of the Lucky Lady Mine?"

"Sure. It's owned by George Bertram and his daughter, Lilly. They're honest and hardworking, but they can't compete with the big mines. Fact is, everybody knows that the big ones are probably working George and Lilly's claim hundreds of feet below their own shaft. Not a damn thing either George or Lil can do to stop them. No proof. They haven't the money to invest and they're too proud to create a corporation and issue stock so that they could raise the capital they so badly need."

"I see. And what about the Montezuma?"

But the sheriff had talked all he was going to talk. "I'm sorry, Miss Starbuck. The Montezuma is one of the oldest

20

and richest of the mines but I can't say much about what it's doing right now. Assay reports and tonnages are closely guarded secrets. You want to know things like that, you'll have to ask Mr. La Fleur. He's the vice president and the man in charge of development."

"I'll ask him tomorrow," Jessie promised. She took the sheriff's hand and shook it firmly. "Ki and I are not ones to invent imaginary motives for murder, but we feel sure that the death of Mr. Dorr was directly related to our earlier conversation and that which would have followed."

The sheriff just shrugged and filed the reports. "Everyone in Virginia City has an opinion on everything, ma'am. You and the samurai are sure entitled to your own. And by the way, Ki. I know full well what you can do with those feet and hands. They're weapons, just as deadly as a knife and a gun. Unless you are pushed to the wall and have no choice, I don't want you to go breaking anyone's arms or legs. A man who can't work up here will starve to death."

"If you know about my skills, you must also know of *kakuto bugei,* the true samurai's way, which says that we never attack, only defend."

The sheriff just grinned. "Like hell you say! When I was sixteen I signed on a frigate bound for the Orient. I spent three months in Japan and China. I've seen what you fellas can do and I'm damned sure you aren't traveling with Miss Starbuck because you can take good dictation. That's why I'm warning you right now to be careful."

Ki bowed slightly at the waist. "A samurai only defends," he repeated.

"Yeah," Slater quipped, "about like a Belgian tiger defends a whole damned jungle."

21

Chapter 3

"Before we go to our hotel, I want to pay a visit to the Lucky Lady Mine," Jessie announced as they started down C Street. "Bill Evans is a man I trust, and he advised me to seek out George Bertram and his daughter. He said that they'd give us the straight of things up here. I'd better hear what they have to say before I begin to negotiate with La Fleur and his friends tomorrow."

It was easy enough to get directions. The Lucky Lady Mine was up near the Divide, a prominent ridge that separated Virginia City from its nearest neighbor and rival, Gold Hill. The Lucky Lady Mine Company headquarters did not look even a little bit lucky to Jessie as they entered the barbed-wire compound with the NO TRESPASSING signs posted everywhere. The headquarters was nothing more than a rusty tin shack which was in such disrepair that Jessie could see through its cracks and hear the ancient steam engine and boiler which operated inside.

"That's far enough!" a voice boomed. "One more step and I'll blow both of you to pieces!"

Jessie squinted into a setting sun. A short old man who looked like he had seen better days had stepped out of the shack and now stood with a shotgun aimed in her and Ki's general direction. Jessie said, "I need to speak to George Bertram. I'm a friend of a friend of his."

23

"I ain't got no friends, pretty lady. Only enemies. So go on and git!"

"The name of our friend is Wild Bill Evans."

Jessie saw a wide smile crease the split lips of the old man, who now lowered his shotgun.

"Wild Bill Evans is still alive?"

"He sure is," Jessie called, breathing a sigh of relief. "He cooks for my roundup crew down on Circle Star Ranch in Texas."

"Old Wild Bill learned how to cook?"

"That's right," Jessie said, daring to raise her hand to shade her eyes. His pants were worn out in both knees, his work boots were shot, and his shirt was faded to a soft blue. He had one of the bushiest silver beards Jessie had ever seen. "Wild Bill sent along a present for you, Mr. Bertram."

The old miner dropped his shotgun in the dirt and shuffled forward. He was crippled up and seemed to move like a gunnysack full of disassociated bones, but he was surprisingly energetic.

"Whaddaya know about that! Old Wild Bill Evans is still alive and cooking for a Texas ranch!" Bertram said over and over to himself. When he reached Jessie, he was as excited as a kid at Christmas. "What did he send fer me?"

Jessie reached into her pocket and handed the man a small package. Bertram ripped the wrapping off of it and his eyes widened. It was an oversized, hand-carved tobacco pipe with an inscription scratched in its stem that read "If you can't smoke this, stick it up your ass and blow bubbles. Yer friend, Wild Bill."

Bertram threw back his head and roared gales of laughter. "That crusty old bastard ain't changed at all, has he!"

Jessie shook her head. Wild Bill was still a great practical joker though he was in his mid-seventies and pretty stiff from rheumatism. "My name is Jessica Starbuck and this is my friend Ki."

Instead of shaking their offered hands, Bertram jammed a wad of Red Dog chewing tobacco into his new pipe and found a match. He lit the pipe and inhaled. The tobacco burned brightly and its acrid smell was guaranteed to be strong enough to keep the evening mosquitoes away. "It smokes real nice," Bertram said with obvious satisfaction. "Wild Bill stold all my pipes when we was mustangers up in Montana. Always said he'd make one special for me. And he kept his word."

Jessie nodded. They chatted for several minutes about nothing in particular and then Jessie got down to business. She asked the old prospector about the Montezuma Mine. His reaction was swift and blunt. "That one is a disaster. Been worked out already. They probably are working pay dirt right under our feet this very minute."

"And there is nothing you can do to stop them in court?"

"Nope. How kin me and Lil prove anything if we can't catch 'em? And to catch 'em, we need to go about three hundred feet straight down."

"I see. Would you consider a silent partner?"

"Hell, no!"

"Why not?" Jessie asked.

"Ain't such a thing. Besides, me and Lil have given this our blood. It's ours and it ain't for sale. Not fer anything."

"I'm sorry to hear that."

Bootsteps crunching along hard rock gravel turned Jessie around. She saw a young woman her own age standing in dusty overalls with work boots, and a miner's lamp on her head. The girl was strong looking but surprisingly pretty, given the dirt smeared on her hands and face. She was wearing baggy men's clothing and her sleeves were

25

rolled up to her elbows to reveal muscular forearms. She had narrow hips, big breasts and thick, work-hardened hands. She was looking at Ki.

"Lil, Lil darlin'," Bertram cried, shoving his smoking pipe at her. " 'Member me tellin' you about old Wild Bill Evans and me in Montana?"

"About a hundred times," Lil said, her broad shoulders relaxing and a smile tugging at the corners of her mouth.

"Well, these here are friends of his and they sent along this here pipe. Lookee what the bastard wrote."

Lil took the pipe and burst out into laughter that was man-sized. "Damn! He sure does have a good sense of humor, don't he!"

Jessie nodded. The young woman was pretty, but she was mighty rough in her ways. But then, Jessie reminded herself, what else could a woman be who was obviously working this mine under her own steam? It was obvious that her father was physically unable to do much in the way of helping her any longer.

"I need to talk to you about mining on the Comstock," Jessie said to the old man. "I want to hire you as a sort of consultant."

"A what?"

"Consultant," Jessie repeated. "A consultant is someone that someone else pays for advice."

"And here I been doing that free all my life!"

"Not today," Jessie said. It was painfully clear that these two could use the money very badly. And when Jessie followed the old man into the headquarters, she was even more shocked to see that the father and daughter were sleeping and eating squeezed in between all the machinery. It was a grim and desperate existence.

"What do I have to tell you, and how much will you pay me?" Bertram asked.

26

Jessie studied the leaking boiler and the machinery, which was rusted and pieced together with wire and a prayer. "I'll pay you a hundred dollars an hour," she told him.

Bertram laughed outright. "I'll settle for a dollar an hour, pretty lady. But what I have to say might not even be worth that much."

Jessie turned to Ki. They had already decided that the samurai should sort of look around, possibly try and learn as much as he could from the daughter about the Comstock Lode, the Montezuma and the Lucky Lady mines in specific. "Why don't you and Lil look around."

Lil seemed to like that idea fine. She studied the tall man and said, "You want to go down and see our mine?"

"Sure," Ki answered.

Lil motioned for her father to lower the cage when they were ready. Ki was not sure what was happening, but he allowed himself to be led forward onto the flooring of the cage.

"Best grab ahold of me, mister," the girl advised. "When Pa lowers this cage, he does it kinda sudden."

Ki took the girl's arm. There were no sides to the cage and he could see through the grating directly under his feet. There was nothing but a dark hole beneath them. "How deep is it?"

"Not deep," she assured him. "Only about a hundred and fifty feet."

It sounded plenty deep to the samurai, and when the old miner threw a lever that allowed the flat cablewire to unwind off a huge spool the cage dropped so suddenly that Ki felt his stomach jump up into his throat as they were hurled down the shaft at almost a free-fall rate of descent. Ki grabbed for something, and the girl was all there was to hang onto. She seemed more than eager to have him in her arms and, had the circumstances been different, he would not have objected to the embrace. She was obviously wearing nothing under her baggy shirt except her skin, and she was laughing so hard her big breasts were shaking.

All at once, the brake went on and the cable whined with a tortured screech. Ki felt as if the floor was being pushed up through his legs. The cage struck the base of the shaft with considerable impact and they were thrown out into a cavern where one flickering candle gave only the vaguest impression of the size of the room.

Ki was furious. It seemed obvious to him that old George Bertram had deliberately dropped the cage at a hair-raising speed simply to frighten one uninitiated samurai.

But he said nothing as he picked himself off the floor of the cavern. Lil did the same. She walked a little unsteadily over to the candle and removed it from the wall. She used its flame to light a kerosene lamp. Suddenly the cavern was completely illuminated. Ki realized that the room was at least fifty feet square and that there were three tunnels leading off in opposite directions.

"This is where we keep the dynamite and tools," Lil explained. "We also sleep down here in the winter, so that's why we have beds and blankets over there. It's warmer down here in winter and cooler in the summer. I like it then, but the rest of the year I'd rather be up on top. I miss the sky, you know."

Ki knew plenty well. He had a slight feeling of claustrophobia and the impassive stone walls that surrounded him seemed to lean in on them. "Where do the tunnels go?"

"Just about twenty feet into the mountain. I've almost been buried a couple of times but we can't afford the shoring that will stop the roof from dropping. Wood is too expensive, at least the kind of timber we need to hold up to the weight."

Lil pointed at one of the tunnels. It was about six feet in diameter and appeared to have been worked the most. "I'm almost sure that one leads to a pocket of gold or silver. Mark my word, if you knew anything about rock I could show you what I mean."

"Show me anyway," Ki said. The samurai knew that Jessie wanted to help these people and she would want to know if the Lucky Lady was really a potential gold mine or just another oversized hole in the ground.

"You sure? It's always a little dangerous," Lil admitted.

"I'd like to see it anyway."

Lil shrugged. "Good enough." She lifted the kerosene lamp and led him into the tunnel.

Ki's claustrophobia increased dramatically but he steeled himself and used his iron-willed mental discipline to quell his rising discomfort. He followed the girl down the tunnel until they came to its end. Ki noticed that the tunnel was shored, but the support seemed entirely insufficient.

"See all this quartz rock?" Lil asked in a subdued tone of voice. "This quartz is the best sign of a gold or silver deposit. Anyone will tell you that. And look here."

They both bent down and the girl took a knife from her pocket and pried loose some rock. "If I take this to the assay office, they'll tell me it is rich ore."

"Then why don't you mine it?"

Lil looked overhead. "Because, without the kind of expensive timbering we need, we'd be signing our own death warrants."

Ki understood completely. The Bertrams needed money to make money. It was a very familiar story. "Can I keep this?"

29

"Sure," she told him. "But it would take a ton of the stuff to make you any real money. A few little rocks like that won't yield enough to buy you a cup of coffee."

"I understand," Ki said. "Shall we leave now?"

Lil was more than ready. She turned and accidentally bumped Ki, who bumped one of the thin little supporting timbers.

"Look out!" Lil cried, dropping the lantern.

Ki felt dirt and gravel began to rain down on them. He looked up and saw the roof starting to move. He grabbed Lil by the arm and jerked her so hard she came right off her feet. Head down, he pulled the young woman down the tunnel, and they threw themselves out into the main cavern just as the roof collapsed.

They lay on the floor hearing tons of rock crashing downward.

Lil gasped. "You saved my life in there!" she whispered.

"Is this cavern safe?" Ki was not afraid of dying like a samurai, one fighting for something worthy. But being buried in a mine cave-in was so utterly meaningless.

"Sure. Ki, I twisted my knee as we were running. Carry me over to the bed and sit me down, please?"

The single candle still flickered and now the samurai's eyes were better adjusted to the dimness.

He picked the girl up and carried her to the rough pine bed and laid her down. He started to stand, but she pulled him down on top of her. "You're the first man who's ever been down here with me alone," she whispered. "I've worked so long alone down here that sometimes I get to thinking the craziest things. Sometimes I've wondered how it would be to have a man a hundred feet below the earth."

Ki relaxed. "What about the knee?"

"I lied," she admitted. "Don't you wonder how it would feel to make love under all this rock?"

"It would feel just the same as it would anywhere. No difference."

She unbuttoned her blouse. "Prove it."

"Now?"

"Sure. We may never have this chance again."

"But we don't even know each other."

"Yes we do. I knew you was the man I wanted down here the second I laid eyes on you. And when you saved my life, it just proved me right. Please?"

Ki knew it was ridiculous. This young woman had been underground too long and maybe she was a little crazy. But she was in need and she was excited and hungry. The samurai decided that it would not be fair to deny her the pleasure of her secret fantasy.

He cupped her breasts and his lips found her nipples. "Tell me," he whispered, "exactly how you wanted it to happen."

"All right. I wanted a man to tear off my pants and rape me."

The samurai's eyebrows lifted questioningly. "Are you sure?"

She was already breathing hard. "Yes," she whispered. "I just wanted him to be hard and fast with me the first time."

Ki smiled as he stood up. "Oh, you mean there's supposed to be a second time?"

She nodded very emphatically. "After the first time, I dreamed he told me he was sorry for being so rough, and then he took me slow and easy, kinda gentle like as if he wanted to make up for being such an animal the first time."

He slipped out of his pants. "So you wanted it both ways—rough, then easy."

31

She stared at his rising manhood and her voice was thick with desire. "Yeah, just like that."

Ki realized he very much wanted to play this game. Nearly being buried by the cave-in only moments before had heightened his senses, and the woman on the bed would be the first he had taken since leaving Texas weeks ago.

"Stand up," he ordered.

Lil stood up. Ki grabbed her shirt and pulled it back over her shoulders as his mouth found first one nipple and then the other. She moaned and he tore her pants open and plunged his hand down into her womanhood. She arched her back and he felt her shiver with delight. Ki pushed her back down on the bed, grabbed her pantlegs, and jerked her pants off over her big workboots. As he had suspected, she was wearing no undergarments and he left her boots on as he shoved her knees apart.

"Oh yes!" she cried. "It was always just like this. Don't stop!"

Ki had no intention of stopping. He was long and hard, and he buried his swollen rod into her eager body with great pleasure. Lil sucked in a sharp breath and he started to pull back thinking he had injured her. But she locked her work boots around his hips and yelled, "Come on, don't stop, dammit, please don't stop!"

Ki's mouth found her breasts. Lil was a very strong woman, and she began to thrust powerfully back at him, to rock and pitch with mounting urgency. Ki found that her animal strength excited him greatly. He was the stronger, but her hunger was equal to his.

"Harder!" she cried. "Harder!"

The samurai gave up the last shred of restraint. He was so well endowed that he had always feared hurting the insides of a woman, but this would not be the case with Lil.

So he began thrusting, his crotch slamming in and out against hers and the faster and harder he went, the more she loved it. All too soon, the moment came when they both lost control. She started to cry out with ecstasy but he covered her mouth with his own as her body spasmed and his hips locked and fed torrents of seed up into her strong young body.

For several minutes, they were too out of breath to speak. She clung to him and in the pale candlelight he could see that her eyelids were shuttered.

"Oh, Ki,"she breathed, "I never had the imagination to dream it could be that good. Not ever!"

He started to rise, but her muscular legs kept him pinioned in place. "You can't quit yet," she begged. "Now comes the slow, gentle way."

Ki sagged against her. He just hoped that George Bertram was as windy as he had appeared to be. Otherwise, Jessie was just going to have to cool her heels up there a little longer than she had expected.

Chapter 4

As they left the Regency Hotel and walked along C Street to meet Andre La Fleur and the other Montezuma Mine executives, Jessie glanced sideways at the samurai. "You sure spent a long time down in that shaft last evening. Even dear old George had about run out of things to say."

Ki's cheeks warmed a little but he managed to keep his eyes straight ahead as he said, "The mine tour was . . . very, very interesting. As I told you, if those rock samples I brought out assay high grade, I think that you might want to consider investing in the Lucky Lady."

"If they'll allow it," Jessie said, still wondering what the samurai had found that interesting down there, other than young Miss Lilly Bertram. When they had come up to the top again, they had both looked disheveled. But when Ki had explained that they had nearly been trapped in a cave-in, it made sense. "It's the father that's stubborn. If the reports turn out well, you might work on Lil a little harder. She's the key."

Ki grinned. "Excellent idea," he said.

Jessie looked at him strangely, and then they both began to laugh. The secret was out. So much the better. The samurai and Jessie had no strings tied to each other, and each had complete freedom to go to bed with whomever they wished whenever they wished.

When they arrived at the address of the meeting place, Jessie took a deep breath and said, "I have a feeling that this is going to be a real hard sell, Ki. Why don't you spare yourself the boredom and look the town over. Listen to the talk. Learn whatever you can, especially this problem of the lack of good and safe timbering. That seems to be the key."

Ki nodded and went on his way. Jessie stepped inside the office and was rushed by the four men she had seen yesterday. They all smiled and bowed and showed her into their office. They were so eager to have her money invested in their silver and gold mine that Jessie felt almost trapped.

"The Montezuma," La Fleur was saying, "is one of the first and greatest mines on the entire Comstock Lode."

"So I understand, Mr. La Fleur, but I'm not buying past performance. Ore mined five years or even five weeks ago means nothing to me. I want to see daily assay reports and tonnages. I want to see your daily labor costs and safety records."

La Fleur seemed to ignore her request, as though it had not registered on his mind. "Now," he continued, "the main shaft drops to a depth of eleven hundred feet. There are also eleven stopes, or levels, each one hundred feet apart. It was at the three-hundred-foot level that—"

Jessie stood up very suddenly. "Mr. La Fleur, gentlemen, I'm afraid I have failed to make my wishes clearly understood. I want your latest reports and I want to see the mine itself."

"You mean actually go down inside of it?" one of the men asked, his expression reflecting his own astonishment and that of his colleagues.

"That is *exactly* what I mean," Jessie said.

"But you can't be serious!" La Fleur protested. "Miss Starbuck. Mines are very dangerous places. As I said, the lowest level of the Montezuma is eleven hundred feet below the earth! Why, I am told that, at that level, billions of tons of pressure are being exerted on the tunnels. Also, the air temperature climbs higher and higher. At the bottom of our mine the temperature is nearly a hundred and twenty degrees. There are hot gases, poisonous gases, and we worry constantly about accidentally tapping scalding hot underwater reservoirs."

"If it's that deadly, then you should not be operating at those depths," she bluntly told them.

"We have no choice."

"Why?"

They looked at each other and La Fleur apparently decided that he had no choice but to confess a big secret. "A lack of sound timbering prevents us from tunneling laterally any great distance. So we keep going straight down."

"And losing men."

La Fleur nodded almost imperceptibly. "Please," he said, "if you insist on going down then do so only a few hundred feet. That's enough to get an idea of what the Montezuma mine is like."

"All right," Jessie said, "I'll compromise by agreeing to an inspection of the seven-hundred-foot level."

La Fleur looked stricken. "The temperature at that level is over a hundred degrees! It is one of our most dangerous levels."

"Is it productive? Do you have a shift of men working there?"

"Yes and yes," La Fleur admitted, "but . . ."

"Then I want to see it," Jessie told the man. "And I'd like you to see it with me." La Fleur almost fainted. His composure nearly cracked and it took every ounce of his will to nod his head up and down.

"Good," Jessie said. "Then why don't we have that won-

37

derful lunch you promised and we can go down right afterward."

La Fleur didn't look hungry anymore.

Jessie had been deep underground before, but this was not South Africa and the rich diamond mines. This was the Comstock, and when they were lowered down in the cage, she saw that they passed level after level with their big work stations. The cage moved down so quickly that the lighted stations were barely visible. They were not much more than breaks in the darkness, fleeting glimpses of men and machinery that passed all too quickly until the next station.

When they came to the seven-hundred-foot level, Jessie was very glad to exit the cage and enter the large station or gallery. She saw perhaps a dozen men, but it seemed to her that they were moving without purpose. She saw miners constantly glancing at her and La Fleur and then trying to look busy.

"Mr. La Fleur," she said as they donned the miner's hats with their candles and reflectors. "Did you send these men down here just to make it look as if there was activity on these levels?"

"Of course not!" La Fleur protested somewhat weakly. "Why should I practice such a deception? For what purpose?"

"I have no idea. But just to prove what you say, let's go down and pay a surprise visit to the tenth level."

La Fleur seemed to stagger. "That's another three hundred feet!"

"Exactly."

"The temperature will be a—"

"You've already explained that to me!" Jessie said in a sharp voice. "I want to see it."

La Fleur's eyes appealed to the mining foreman, Don

38

Hyer, beside him. Hyer said, "Miss Starbuck, the tenth level isn't safe."

"Cave-ins?"

"Yes."

"Then the ninth."

The foreman shook his head. "Same with the ninth and the eighth stations. To be real honest, there hasn't been a great deal of work on this level lately. We hit a pocket of wet clay. When it dries it expands, and that can cause big trouble with weak shoring."

Jessie looked up. "Is this the famous square-set timbering arrangement I've heard about?"

The foreman nodded. "Yes, it is. It all amounts to nothing more than a series of wooden boxes, one set right next to the other to form these galleries at each level. Then they're extended down the drifts and—"

"The what?"

"Drifts," he explained. "You'd call them tunnels. We shoot them along the sides of the vein. They're generally run in solid rock if we can find it. We call hard rock 'country rock,' and it can't have any lime in it so that it stands hard and won't swell when we expose it to hot air."

"I want to go down one of these drifts," Jessie said, looking at the dark tunnels that radiated out from the huge gallery or station where they stood.

The foreman looked at La Fleur, who just nodded. "Go ahead," he sighed. "She is bound and determined to see it."

"I better get the men to lead the way," the foreman said. "There will be some fallen rock and timber to clear first."

La Fleur appeared ready to quit. He was sweating profusely and a good deal of that was caused by pure fear as well as the heat.

"Why don't you remain here by the cage and wait?" Jessie suggested.

La Fleur wanted to accept that suggestion but something in him refused. He shook his head and raised his chin proudly. "No!" he cried. "I will go ahead. I would not send my men into a tunnel that wasn't safe."

"Are you sure?"

"Yes." La Fleur angrily stomped forward. "Let's go!"

The mine foreman looked worried. He grabbed the sleeve of one of his men and said, "You keep an eye on him. Don't let him get into any trouble down here."

The miner nodded. He was thin and, in the candlelight, his face was sallow and weary.

They started into the drift, which had a gradual rise to it so that ore wagons could be moved easily down to the main shaft where the ore was loaded on the cage and then hoisted to the surface. But as they walked along, feet knocking hollowly on the rock floor, pale headlamps barely penetrating the eerie darkness up ahead, Jessie could see that a heavy layer of dust and silt covered the tracks, and that they appeared not to have been used in months, perhaps even longer.

The drift was not very large, and they kept coming to even smaller tunnels that intersected it.

"What are these called?" Jessie asked.

"Crosscuts, Miss Starbuck. 'Member how I said we run these bigger drifts along a likely looking vein?"

"Yes."

"Well, these crosscuts intersect the vein. We send them out every hundred feet or so to do what we call 'prospect' the vein. See if it has anything. As you can plainly see, these crosscuts also have ore-cart rails."

Jessie nodded. She could see places where the earth had broken away from the roof and crashed to the floor. "You need more timbering overhead."

"Yes, ma'am. But when it ain't available, or it's so ex-

40

pensive that you either risk your life and go without it or shut down and starve, then you take the risk. I'm surprised that Mr. La Fleur even dared to come down here with us, much less get his back up and lead the way. A poor miner, well, he has no choice, but Mr. La Fleur?"

Jessie understood the foreman very well. These miners often had wives and children to support, and if they refused to work in an unsafe drift, then there would be plenty of other men willing to take the risk.

"How many men are dying each week on the Comstock from cave-ins?" she asked.

"About ten a week, Miss Starbuck. But there's thousands more just waiting for the chance to take their jobs."

Jessie shook her head sadly. This looked like a death-trap for certain And if—

"Look out!" she heard a miner scream. "She's coming down!"

The foreman grabbed Jessie and jerked her completely off her feet as he whirled and began to run back down the drift toward the station. Jessie heard shouts, more screams, and then the terrible sound of tons of rock crashing down into the drift. A huge blast of air and dust overtook them, enveloped them, and sent them flying even faster like leaves being pushed by the front of a powerful storm.

Jessie fell, lost her useless headlamp, picked herself up again in the swirling, choking darkness, and raced on. And on. Finally, she burst into the station behind the foreman, who was still racing for the cage. Overhead, dirt and rocks began to rain down on them and Jessie felt herself being pelted.

"Into this cage!" the foreman shouted, grabbing a signal bell and pulling on it frantically for the operator up on top to raise the cage.

Jessie leapt into the cage. "But the others!" she screamed.

41

"There are no others!" the foreman bellowed. "There can't be anyone left."

Jessie carried a concealed derringer and she drew it out and placed it to the foreman's head. "Signal again for the man up on top to wait!" she screamed.

The foreman signaled and the cage, which had begun to lift, stopped and dangled three feet above the level of the station's floor as the earth shook and they listened to mighty timbers snap and pop all around them like twigs.

"It's all going to come down on us, I tell you!" the foreman shouted. "There are *no* survivors!"

A huge rock struck the cage and knocked it sideways so that it swung back and forth, banging the sides of the shaft. Jessie fell hard and the foreman grabbed her and pulled her to her feet. More rocks began to fall, striking the roof of the cage, threatening to break it free from its cable and send it spinning down the shaft.

The foreman signaled up the bell rope again, and this time Jessie did not try to stop him. The earth seemed to be collapsing all around them in the terrifying darkness.

"Up!" the foreman shouted. "Up, damn you!"

As if in answer to their prayers, the cage was jerked through the roof of the collapsing station. A deafening roar filled the shaft and a mighty rush of air and dust shot upward, overtaking the fleeing cage and almost asphyxiating them.

It seemed like hours before the cage slammed out of the bowels of Sun Mountain and Jessie and the foreman were ripped away by the hands of men. It seemed to Jessie as if she had just been delivered from hell itself.

Chapter 5

The body of Andre La Fleur was packed into a hearse wagon alongside two other men. The remaining five bodies had been buried far back in the Montezuma Mine, and the drift had been boarded up. Their bodies would never be recovered. Jessie, Ki, and the families of the dead men walked to the cemetery to hear a minister deliver a very brief and uninspired sermon.

As Jessie stood on the sun-baked hillside and tried to concentrate on the minister's words, it struck her that the families of the dead miners were more than grief-stricken, they were also fatalistic. Even the minister indicated that, on the Comstock Lode, the chances of a miner living out his natural life span were practically nil. He said, "Oh, Lord, Thou did not mean for man to be underground, but let these men we consign to Your mercy and love be forgiven, because they were only trying to feed their families. We pray that the rock Thou has made this terrible mountain of will harden, so that fewer and fewer men are called to Thy side at such a young age. And most of all, we pray for the families of the dead, that Thou would give them the courage and the wisdom to know that this is Thy plan and Thy will be done, forever and ever."

Jessie studied the families. She saw little children and wives that looked so very poor. When the brief funeral

43

service ended, she and Ki declined a ride and remained with the poor families as they walked down the hot, dusty road to Virginia City. Entering the offices of the Montezuma Mine Company, Jessie asked to see one of La Fleur's executives.

The man's name was Mr. Johnson. When he saw Jessie, he somehow summoned up a dazzling smile. "Well, Miss Starbuck! Welcome. I . . . we, well, we are surprised to see you and your friend. We naturally assumed that after the cave-in you would decide not to pursue further negotiations with us on the purchase of the Montezuma. But we are delighted to—"

"You assumed right," Jessie said quite abruptly. It amazed her that these people could be so insensitive as to suggest that they talk business on the very day after eight Montezuma employees had been crushed. "I'm not the least bit interested in buying your mine."

Johnson blinked and the smile slipped badly. "Then why are you here?" he asked in a strained voice.

"I want you to inform the families of those who died on the seventh level yesterday that there is a check waiting for them, a check in memory of their husbands and fathers, on deposit in the Nevada Commerce Bank on B Street. But I must ask that you do not reveal that I was the donor."

Johnson raised his chin. "Miss Starbuck, some of the men who died yesterday had families, some did not."

Jessie nodded. "The bank has been instructed to donate a thousand dollars per dependent and an equal sum for the single men to the Miners' Relief Fund here in Virginia City."

"That's exceedingly generous of you."

Jessie turned away. She did not feel generous at all, only saddened, and determined that she would drive a few morticians out of business before she was finished. If there

44

was good timber to be had up at Lake Tahoe, she would do whatever was required to get it to Virginia City as soon as possible and sell it reasonably, even if it meant doing so at a loss.

"Miss Starbuck, may I be candid with you?"

"Of course."

Johnson motioned her and Ki into his office and closed the door behind them. "I am aware that the Territorial Enterprise intends to interview you concerning this latest tragedy. It would be a further disaster and hardship on everyone concerned with the Montezuma Mine Company if you or Mr. Ki said anything about what happened on our seven-hundred-foot level."

"Why?" Jessie leaned forward with interest. She was quite sure that she knew why, but she wanted to hear Johnson put it into words and confirm her suspicions.

He shifted uncomfortably. "Well, it would be terrible publicity. You see, if the deaths of those men were misinterpreted as negligence or . . . or in some way our fault, it could result in expensive litigation and a precipitous drop in the value of our company's stock."

Jessie's suspicions were confirmed and she reacted strongly. "I think that you and your company are frauds, Mr. Johnson. I think that those drifts down below are death-traps. You and this company have been losing money and so you have cut costs for even the barest level of timbering. It's my opinion that you and Montezuma should be prosecuted to the fullest extent possible under the laws for gross negligence."

Johnson shook his head back and forth. "That's not true!"

"Isn't it?" Ki demanded. "While Jessie was down in your mine yesterday, I did a little investigating. It wasn't hard to learn that you and this company have been shipping

45

low-grade ore to a stamp mill down on the Carson River and paying the operators of that mill to falsify the assay reports. You've been doing that to keep your worthless stock bouyed up while you quietly sell before it crashes. Isn't that true?"

Johnson shook his head violently. "No!" he hollered. "That's a lie!"

"I pity you and the other officers," Jessie said. "Mr. La Fleur gambled desperately and lost. He was rushing ahead with several of his men in order to plant some gold or silver at the face of the tunnel so that I would pick it up, have it assayed, and believe that the mine was still rich. Isn't that true?"

"Get out of here!" Johnson shouted. "Out!"

Jessie motioned to Ki that they should leave, but she stopped at the door and said, "I'll tell the Territorial Enterprise exactly what I have just stated. Within two hours, this company will be bankrupt and the Montezuma Mine abandoned. My only regret is that I know that we'll never be able to prove that it was Montezuma that sent a killer up to shadow us from Carson City. When your overzealous assassin heard Mr. Dorr begin to talk about how the mines on the Lode were in danger of being shut down because of lack of timber, the killer panicked. Thinking that you would want to have Dorr silenced before he scared off a potential buyer, the killer murdered Mr. Dorr."

"You can't prove any of that!"

Jessie's eyebrows raised. "Don't bet on it, Mr. Johnson."

The man swallowed and fear crept into his eyes. Jessie was bluffing, but Johnson and his peers could not afford to take the chance of it and be caught up in a murder trial.

"What do you want from us?" Johnson shouted. "Our blood?"

Jessie considered the question. The Montezuma Mine Company was situated right over the great vein of gold and silver that ran north and south down Six Mile Canyon. True, the mine had been completely unsuccessful in tapping that vein that geologists said ran in pockets, like strings of beads. But there was no reason to assume that luck would not change in the near future, and that the Montezuma would again become highly profitable. It desperately needed heavy timbering and capital. If she told the Territorial Enterprise of her suspicions, she would indeed ruin Johnson and a few of his fellow officers, but she would also be throwing a lot of good men out of work.

"I will remain silent if you sell me your stock and that of every other officer in the mine for ten thousand dollars."

"What! My stock alone is worth seventy thousand on today's market."

Jessie shrugged her shoulders. "After my interview, I doubt very much that it will be worth anything at all. Take it or leave it. Consider it your travel money off the Comstock Lode."

Johnson pulled out a handkerchief and mopped his face. "You are without a heart," he whispered.

"I have a heart filled with compassion for the working men who have died because of your miserly ways. Take my offer or leave it."

"I...I will have to discuss this with my board members. Our combined stock would exceed a quarter of a million dollars. By buying it at ten thousand, you stand to make a small fortune."

"Yes," Jessie said, "but I'll put every penny of it into the effort to bring timber to the Comstock and save lives."

Johnson nodded. He suddenly looked defeated. "I want out of this nightmare," he said.

Jessie looked at the man and nodded. "I give you and

every other officer one hour to divest yourself of your stock and give me your answer."

Johnson swallowed. "Mr. La Fleur said you were too beautiful to be smart or ruthless in business. He said we could eat you alive. But you've just eaten all of us. You're like a beautiful alligator, Miss Starbuck."

Jessie had been called many things during tough, protracted negotiations for properties around the world, but this was a first. "Maybe, but at least I am not a party to murder."

Jessie found herself the principal owner of the Montezuma Mine. She and Ki inspected each level and ordered the crews not to work below the four-hundred-foot level until the lower drifts could be resupported with good timber. She kept her promise and did not speak to the Territorial Enterprise of her suspicions, and before she left the Comstock she asked all of the Montezuma miners to assemble.

They were a hard-looking crew numbering almost fifty men. At one time the Montezuma had employed three shifts numbering over a hundred and forty. As she looked at the miners, she felt certain that they expected to be laid off. Some had their families in attendance and the mood was grim.

"Gentlemen," she said, causing more than a few smiles, "I know the situation down below is unsafe beyond the fourth level, and we are shutting it down. I want you to keep working on the second, third and fourth levels and extend the crosscuts, so long as they do not go under anyone else's claim."

"What if we already are?" a miner asked.

"Then board the drift up and start a new one from the station. I won't have us stealing another man's gold or silver, not even if he can't reach it. I want safety to be the

48

number-one concern down below. Profits are important, but safety comes first. Is that understood by everyone?"

The miners and their families looked absolutely dumbfounded. They acted as if they could not believe their ears. All their working lives underground, management had not shown the slightest interest in their lives, and now here was someone saying that safety came first. It didn't compute.

"Miss Starbuck," one of the miners spoke up. "Maybe you don't know the whole truth of this here mine, but we ain't been finding any high-grade ore in months. That's why we're on a skeleton crew. The mine is losin' money."

Jessie smiled. "Thank you for your honest appraisal, sir. But the fact is I have a little money to gamble and I expect the losses to continue for a while. But every geologist's report I've read says that the Comstock Lode hasn't yet begun to be tapped. I think that the Montezuma Mine will produce another fortune before this is all said and done. I'm willing to bet on it."

One miner actually pinched his cheek to make sure he was awake and not dreaming. Others just grinned.

Jessie continued, "I intend to find a way to bring good Sierra timber to this mine and to the other mines. It's definitely the key. To that end, I and my friend will be leaving for Lake Tahoe at once. We should be getting timbering here before the end of this month. In the meantime, safety is all-important."

Jessie and Ki left them and walked swiftly to the waiting horses they had bought for the ride to Tahoe. They were leaving Virginia City behind for a short while. As she mounted, Jessie heard the sharp, strident blasts of the V and T Railroad locomotive coming up from Carson City and she was reminded of poor Ethan Dorr. She would never have been able to prove that the Montezuma Mine Company was behind the man's murder. Very likely, the murderer had been working under the orders of La Fleur, a cold-hearted little fish if ever there was one.

They rode up C Street and crossed over the Divide to ride down through Gold Hill and Silver City. The road down the canyon was filled with ore wagons and miners. They heard piano music and men singing as their picks struck the rock. Jessie shook her head with amazement. She had never seen anything quite the equal of the Comstock Lode. On the surface it appeared as if everything was well and good, but underneath, mines were collapsing and men were being buried alive.

Jessie touched spurs to the flanks of the horse she rode. The animal quickened its pace as she and Ki began to weave in and out of the line of ore and freight wagons. They had a long way to go before they reached Tahoe. It would be cool and green and Jessie remembered that the water was as clear as glass.

It would seem like another world. A much kinder one.

Chapter 6

Sunset caught them on the rim of the Sierras, and the view of Lake Tahoe was breathtaking. The huge lake lay bathed in crimson and pink, like the bejeweled pendant of a goddess, cast down from the heavens to rest in the striking green of heavy forest. Beyond the lake, snow-capped mountains paraded majestically to the north and south as far as the eye could see.

"I've traveled the world," Jessie said, dismounting to let her weary horse blow after the long climb up from the Carson Valley behind them, "but this is my favorite alpine lake. It has such pristine beauty that I wish it could never be touched."

Ki also dismounted. "How does that fit against your plans for logging?" he asked.

Jessie thought about it for several moments before speaking. "There are millions of trees up here, Ki. The way to do it is to log those that are old or dying. In the Pacific Northwest, that's the way they log so that their forests will never be cut down. By thinning the sick or old trees, sunlight can filter down to the earth and the young saplings can have a chance to grow and become new forests."

"That must add a great deal to the cost of lumber."

Jessie had to admit the samurai had a point. Selective

51

thinning of forests was considerably more expensive in the short run, even though it did ensure that there would be good timber available for future generations. "We'll find a way," she told Ki.

It amused the samurai how Jessie was always talking about how each of her many world-wide enterprises was expected to carry its own weight and show a profit. And yet, when it came to things like conservation or keeping poor miners safely employed, profit meant nothing. Jessie Starbuck was a paradox, a woman who worked very hard to show men that she deserved to be counted their equal in any boardroom on any continent. At the same time, she was too much of a humanitarian to allow strict accounting to determine her choice of action. To Ki's way of thinking, Jessie used the perfect combination of heart and cold capitalist reason.

They remounted and headed toward the lake. The sun eased down on the rim of the world like a monstrous red ball of fire. As it slowly disappeared, Lake Tahoe's brilliant colors softened, then gradually faded into a soft gray-blue, and Ki saw the first evening star over California.

They had not purchased bedrolls, for there were a number of small hotels and cabins to rent rooms in for the night. Most of them were down on the south shore of the lake, but Ki suspected that they would come upon some before then. The road they followed was wide, and was used heavily by ore and supply wagons. With any luck at all, they would find good lodgings within the hour.

But he was wrong. After another hour had passed the moon had grown full, and Jessie decided they should continue on to the lakeside. "I want to walk beside it at day-break," she confided. "Perhaps we can catch a breakfast of cold-lake trout."

Ki approved of the idea. He too had been here before,

and the water was so clear that a man could see forty or fifty feet down and actually watch huge fish as they swam along the bottom searching for food. Because of the water's purity and coldness, the meat of the trout was firm, pink, and entirely delicious. It would be a nice way to start the day.

"If we don't find lodging, we can always make a dry camp beside the lake. It won't get that cold tonight," Jessie said.

Ki wasn't sure about that. Even though it was summer, at over six thousand feet of elevation the nights could get bitingly cold. He was not worried about his own discomfort, but that of Jessie.

"Did you have mountains like these in Japan?"

"Mount Fuji-San," Ki said, "is over twelve thousand feet. Japan has many mountains. Very beautiful mountains."

"Like these?"

"No," the samurai said. "They are different. Everything in America is different than in Japan."

"Including the people."

"Especially the people."

"Do you ever wish to go back and live there?" Jessie looked at her samurai. "You could, you know. I would miss you terribly, but I'd never want to think that I held you."

"Texas and your Circle Star Ranch is my home now."

Jessie nodded. "It's just that the ranch is in such arid, hard country. Sometimes, when I compare it to Japan where you were raised, it seems . . ."

Ki frowned. "Beauty is relative. To a prospector who spends his life in the American desert, there is beauty to be found all around him. In the cactus, in the small desert flowers, and in the harsh gray of the sage and brush. To

53

someone else, this mountain country is most beautiful. I choose not to compare one kind of beauty with another. The earth is all beautiful, Jessie. In some places, you might have to look harder to really see the beauty, but it is there."

Jessie shook her head. "It would take a samurai to see beauty in the middle of a sandy desert. To me, the mountains are most beautiful."

"Then perhaps we should live here. With your money, you could buy a great stretch of lake shore and live here instead of in Texas."

"Don't be ridiculous," she told him. "What would I do with our herds of longhorn cattle? Feed them pine cones?"

Ki just grinned. He was never entirely sure whether Jessie was simply teasing him or actually being serious. In this case, he would give her the benefit of the doubt and assume that she was teasing.

They passed a number of lodges, but they were all full and so they continued on down to the lake. By now the hour was late, so Ki and Jessie chose a small, sandy beach beside the water where there were trees close by. The samurai collected fallen wood and quickly made a campfire on the beach while Jessie hobbled the horses and arranged things. Then she went down to the water and bathed quickly.

"It's even colder than I remembered," she said when she returned to the fire, shivering and brushing her washed hair as it dried.

Ki laid his head back against his saddle and pulled his horseblanket over his body. He stared up at the starry heavens and thought back to his childhood in Japan. His memories were a collage of pain and sadness. His mother had fallen in love with a tall, dashing American seaman though this incurred the displeasure of her royal family. The Japanese believed that anyone outside of their race was inferior, and so when Ki's mother had chosen to marry the American, she had been cast out as if she had never been born. Ki's mother had not cared, for she had been so much in love. Her strong, handsome American husband was going to take her and her infant son away where they would live in another land. But then tragedy had struck, and Ki's father had died.

Ki could not remember his father, nor even his mother's pain. She had so loved the American that she had soon died of heartbreak. Perhaps if her family had relented, shown some compassion . . . but of course, Japanese tradition had been violated and they could never have forgiven a daughter for committing such a travesty.

Ki, being half Caucasian and half Oriental, was in a terrible predicament. His height and Caucasian features were like a flag that shouted his mother's great sinfulness. He became a homeless waif. A starving child of the streets, a begger, a thing to be despised and kicked and beaten like a dog. Ki would never forget those early years of his childhood. He had almost come to believe that he was subhuman, a shameful thing not deserving of comfort, of food, a home, a family, even of life itself.

And then he had met the great *ronin* Kobi-san.

In Japanese, *ronin* meant a wave man, a samurai without a master and, therefore, a man without any purpose in life. Kobi-san had been sitting eating out of a bowl when Ki had first crawled up and begged for food. The old *ronin* had slapped him aside and finished his meal. Ordinarily, Ki would have dragged himself away, but by then he was so famished and so ready to die that the prospect of having his head lopped off by the samurai's great *katena*, or long sword, caused no fear to him.

So he had challenged the samurai, the *ronin* whose own life was no longer lived with honor now that his master was dead. And Kobi-san had seen his courage and had relented. He had fed Ki, first food to keep him alive, then his great tradition and code of honor. *Kakuto bugei*, "the true samurai's way," was the code that Kobi-san had given Ki during the last years of the *ronin*'s life. He had even managed to convince Ki that he was worthy of life, but only if he possessed a samurai's unwavering code of honor. Kobi-san taught Ki *te*, the art of empty-hand fighting, in which one's body becomes the ultimate weapon. *Te* was developed by the Okinawans centuries earlier after they had been conquered by the Japanese, and had suffered the indignity of not being allowed to keep their weapons. Without weapons, the Okinawans were thought to be a slave people, but they developed *te* and became their own terrible weapons.

Such was life and the rules of men and warfare. Kobi-san had once explained that it was the mind that was the greatest weapon of all. He would say, "Walls can be a fortress or a prison; which will you chose?"

When Ki's education had been completed, when the young samurai had finished his training, when he had learned how to handle the sword, the bow and arrows, the joined *nunchaku* sticks which would break a man's bones more easily than a hammer, when he had learned *atemi*, the art of applying pressure to a man's arteries and thus turning his mind to sleep, when all of the skills had been mastered to the *ronin*'s exacting standards, then Hirata had said, "In you I took on the last true pupil. In you I have turned the wheel of life into one complete circle. Now that I have taught you all I know, you must go to America, where your father was born. To remain in this land would always bring you pain and disgrace."

Beside him, Jessie reached out and touched his arm. "Ki, are you thinking of Hirata tonight?"

"Yes," he whispered. "How did you know?"

She took his hand and held it tightly. "I just knew," she told him in her soft, gentle voice.

Ki smiled up at the stars. Samurai were bound to protect their masters even if they despised them. Ki breathed deeply of the pine-scented air. He knew he was a very, very fortunate samurai to have someone like Jessie Starbuck to honor and protect.

Morning found Jessie and the samurai fishing off the rocks. There were three big trout beside the samurai, but none resting next to Jessie. She was scowling, clearly disgusted with her lack of success. "I don't know why I even bother to fish. I ought to let you do it for me."

The samurai only smiled.

"What is it you do that I don't?" Jessie asked peevishly. "We have same kind of line, same hooks, same bait, same willow switches for poles. Why can't I ever catch fish the way you do?"

Ki looked over at her and decided that she was serious. She really wanted to know. "You have no patience," he said.

"What!"

"You jerk your line too soon whenever you think you have a nibble. You wiggle around on the rock too much, and your moving shadow scares the fish from your bait. You keep lifting your bait in and out of the water because you think it might have fallen off or gotten eaten. You—"

"Enough!" Jessie cried. "All right! You catch the fish, I'll clean and cook them."

"I'll catch and clean them," Ki said. "If you cook them."

"It's a deal."

Jessie stood up and went to build a fire. Even before it

was smoking really well, Ki was back with four big fishes. They were cleaned and ready. "I'm starving," Jessie told him, realizing that neither of them had eaten dinner the night before.

Ki was hungry as well. Since they had no grate or frying pan, he used the willow poles to skewer the fishes, and they placed them over a small rock ring to cook. All that was required was to turn them over the coals and then enjoy.

"Think they're ready?" Jessie asked eagerly a short time later.

"I think so." The samurai reached for the sticks.

Suddenly, a pair of rifles boomed, and the roasted fishes exploded over the fire. Ki dropped the stick and pivoted, but when he saw two men not thirty yards away by the trees with their rifles pointed and ready to fire, he went still.

Jessie wasn't wearing her gun, and she was furious at herself. Hands on hips, she yelled, "What in the devil do you think you're up to?"

The pair were twins. Both were in their early- to mid-twenties, both long and lank and mean looking. They had brown hair, brown eyes, and thin, scraggly beards. They looked unwashed, and yet they were astride fine horses and custom-made saddles. Their outfits were the best that money could buy, but they still managed to look slovenly.

They didn't move but kept their rifles trained on Jessie and Ki. "You're trespassing on our land!"

Jessie could not believe this. "We crossed no fences and you've posted no signs!"

"Sure we did. Just a couple hundred yards back from the lake. This is all private property. You let your horses eat our grass, and you were fixin' to eat our fish."

Jessie stomped her boot down hard. "This may be your

land, but I'll be damned if the fish in this lake wear your brand. You had no right to shoot them just now!"

One of the brothers turned to the other brother. "Regular bitch hellcat, ain't she, Fred?"

"Damn right she is. Pretty too."

"Too skinny."

"No she ain't. She's got tits even bigger'n Annie's." He waved the barrel of his Winchester at Jessie. "Pull that jacket aside and show us your chest, woman."

Ki was wearing his leather vest, and his hand slipped inside to one of the pockets where he carried *shuriken* star-blades.

"No," Jessie said in a small voice. "I don't want you to kill them unless they push us to the wall."

The samurai's hand moved away from the deadly blades.

"Arnie wants to see the size of your tits, lady! Didn't you hear him order you to pull back your jacket? You don't have to open up your shirt or nothing. We can tell good enough without violating your honor."

"Hell," Arnie admitted, "I'd like to violate her honor plenty. What's your name, woman? And who's the Chink with ya? You didn't sleep with it, did ya?"

Jessie forced herself to grow quiet inside. She had often met these kind of men. They needed to be taught a lesson, but not to be killed unless they got physical. "We're going to forget what you've done to our fish. We'll saddle our horses and ride off your land. But if you keep pushing us you'll be very sorry. So put those rifles away and ride off."

The two brothers gaped at her audacity. "Fred, did you hear that lady ordering us to ride off our own land?"

"I did for a fact," Arnie said. "If that ain't a son of a bitch of a thing for a woman to say. Here she and this Chink spend the night on our land, they catch our fish, their horses eat our grass, and they burn our firewood . . . and she tells us to ride off!"

Jessie sighed. "I don't think they're going to leave us alone, Ki. But try not to kill them."

The samurai nodded. He had been through this before, but this pair seemed particularly bent on their own destruction. "Jessie, let's try and get them to drop their guard and come within reach."

Jessie nodded. She did not like the looks of these two, and she knew that they were capable of killing and raping if they had the chance. And while Ki could have gotten one of them with his *shuriken* blade, if they were good with those Winchesters, the other might have killed him before she could reach her own six-gun.

She had to distract them fully. "Who's Annie?" she asked.

The twins were thrown off guard by the question. Then they both laughed. The one named Arnie said, "She's a whore my pa keeps at our ranch. She cleans the place and keeps us happy whenever we can't find nothin' better to diddle. How are you at cleaning house? We'll fire fat-ass Annie and you kin take her place. How you like that idea, Fred?"

Fred liked it a lot. He dismounted and though he did not shove his rifle back in its saddle scabbard, he held it loosely while his brother watched with a look of anticipation and amusement.

"Whatcha gonna do to her, Fred?"

"I gotta see how big her tits are," he yelled. "Keep your eye on the Chink."

"Aw, he ain't nothing to worry about."

Fred was smiling as he swaggered forward. He was even taller than Jessie had first thought, and there was a lean, catlike movement to him that was definitely predatory. Up close, she could see that the man was closer to thirty than to twenty.

"Better try and wound Arnie," Jessie whispered.

Fred stopped in front of her and raised the barrel of the Winchester until it was inches away from Jessie's chest. "Take your jacket off," he ordered.

"You're making a real mistake, Fred. Why don't you and your brother put those guns away and let us ride off your land without any trouble."

"Sometimes we like trouble, pretty woman. So do as I say."

Jessie removed her jacket. Her heart began to thump faster. Out of the corner of her eye she saw the samurai again reach into his vest pocket, but Arnie was so intent on seeing her expose her breasts that he wasn't even watching Ki.

"Now, pretty thing, unbutton your shirt."

"You said you weren't going to dishonor me," Jessie told the man.

"I lie a hell of a lot, miss. Unbutton the shirt and open it wide."

Jessie shook her head. "No."

Fred licked his lips and stepped forward. "You do as I say and I won't even touch you any. Not unless you want me to. If you been sleeping with a Chink, you must need a man pretty damn bad."

Fred reached out to her. That was the moment Jessie had been waiting for. She brought her knee up hard between his legs with every intention of smashing his testicles. And she must have succeeded because the man screamed with agony at the very moment that Ki's hand shot forward and the *shuriken* blade whistled through the air. It struck Arnie in the shoulder and the rifle in his hands

61

exploded sideways as his horse shied and unseated him. Arnie hit the ground hard yelling with pain.

Ki sent a sweep-kick that had the force of a sledgehammer. It caught Fred in the side of his knee, and the man collapsed in a sea of pain. All visions of Jessie's lush breasts had vanished from his mind.

Jessie took the writhing man's weapons while Ki moved over to retrieve his *shuriken* blade from Arnie's shoulder. The man was red-eyed with hate and pain. "I'll kill you next time, Chink!" he screamed.

Ki grabbed the man by the throat, knowing he could crush Arnie's voicebox and forever silence the fool.

"Ki, no!"

The samurai's powerful fingers relaxed, and he pushed the throat away from him. He gathered the brothers' rifles as well as their six-guns and hurled them far out into the lake.

"You broke my goddamn knee!" Fred screamed. "Pa will have you nailed to a pine tree and castrated for this!"

"We'll be around," Jessie said. "And the next time we see either of you, it will go worse."

"You don't know who the hell you're dealin' with. We're the Yoders! My pa, Clinton, owns this lake."

"No he doesn't," Jessie said. "And I intend to log here."

"You're as good as dead," Arnie whispered. "Both of you!"

Jessie and the samurai quickly saddled their horses and rode away. They did not look back. The lovely view of Lake Tahoe had suddenly lost its charm.

"Did you break his knee?" she asked when they had ridden several miles in cold silence.

"No, but I think I should have," the samurai declared.

Jessie took a deep breath. They had left the two brothers in agony. Neither would die, but sometime, somewhere near this lake, she was dead certain that she and Ki would have to face all the Yoders. And if the old man was anything like his sons, it was not going to be a pleasant reunion.

This was, Jessie ruefully concluded, a damned poor way to start off at Lake Tahoe.

Chapter 7

Scotty's Half Way House was the place where the rugged teamsters who freighted supplies around the southern end of Lake Tahoe from California down to Pine Bluff and Mormon Station generally stopped for a meal and a bed. The establishment was impressive, with its two stories enclosing more than ten thousand square feet. Scotty's Half Way House served as a combination general store, hotel, restaurant, and saloon. Old Scotty had been one of the few California Forty-Niners to strike it rich and then have the wisdom to invest his winnings in something lasting and profitable. The man was famed for his generosity toward destitute miners and teamsters.

When Ki and Jessie walked into his establishment, Scotty was tending bar in his saloon, which proudly boasted a teakwood bar imported from a British officers' club in either Bombay or Calcutta—Scotty kept mixing them up, though he was sure it was someplace in India. Over the bar, which was inlaid with ivory figures of elephants, naked women, and snakes, Scotty happily poured French champagne and English bitter ale for those who figured they owed themselves the very best. In truth, most of Scotty's friends and the stream of teamsters who patronized his bar drank rotgut whiskey and steamer beer. Yet if they were truly busted, Scotty would cheerfully serve them flagons of wine so coarse that even the grape skins and pieces of the plant itself had not been strained off; you could get drunk on fermenting wine free at the Half Way House, but you'd have a hangover so awesome that sensible men showed restraint.

"Well, what do we have here!" Scotty boomed. "A beautiful woman and a tall Chinaman! As I live and breathe, I never know what to expect to come waltzing through my door. Step up to the finest bar in these here Sierra Nevada Mountains, and have a glass of French champagne on Scotty!"

Jessie nodded with a smile, but Ki remained impassive. He always felt insulted when some fool called him a Chinaman, but unless they began to make an issue of race, Ki had trained himself to ignore their ignorance.

"Thank you," Jessie said.

Scotty poured them each a water glass of the bubbly champagne, then poured one for himself. "To your health and my generosity," he said, raising his glass and winking at Jessie.

They drank, and then Jessie said, "That was excellent champagne."

"Chateau Vissy-something or other. Bottled in 1852, the year of my own great good fortune. I bought a hundred cases of it right off the docks of San Francisco, and had two men with rifles guard every drop until it reached my wine cellar. It's got class, miss, same as you."

Jessie blushed a little at the compliment and the man's bold gaze. Scotty had to be in his early seventies, but he had a roguish look and a twinkle in his eye. He did not act his age but instead that of a man thirty years younger.

"You and the Chinaman just passing through to California?"

"He's not a Chinaman," Jessie was obliged to say. "He's

half American, half Japanese. He's a samurai."

Scotty just shrugged. Apparently, he was not interested in knowing what a samurai was, for he continued, "I think he looks like a Yosemite Indian. They was pretty well wiped out by the Forty-Niners, you know."

Jessie said, "We want to start a logging operation on the lake."

"You and him?" Scotty asked, not bothering to hide his amazement. "You and the samurai have just decided you want to log timber around the shores of Lake Tahoe?"

"Yes."

"Old Clinton Yoder would change your mind about that in a hurry, miss. Clinton has run off or killed everyone who had a mind to log along the shores of this lake. It ain't right, nor legal, nor anything else, but that's the way of things up here."

"What about the law?"

"There ain't no law. For a couple of months during the year, the snow is so damned deep that nothing moves anyways except to seek the warmth of the Sacramento Valley. I stay here because I have to. If I left, thieves would carry off everything in the place. Otherwise I'd get off the mountain for the winter."

"Does the lake freeze?"

"Only around the edges, and then not very thick or long. Wind gets pretty fierce, though. You heard about what happened to the Donner Party not so many years ago. Only about forty miles north, just above the lake."

Jessie knew full well of that great tragedy, and had no wish to get into a discussion on it. "This Clint Yoder, does he log in the wintertime?"

"Yep. He's cutting timber all year around. Course, he has built himself a skid road that he uses. In clear weather, he just hitches up oxen and drags logs to the skid road and then lets them slide on down to the Carson River. But he's got a sawmill about ten miles upshore on the California side, and he uses that to make lumber. Most of it he sells in Sacramento. The man is getting rich and he owns some timber stands along the shore, though not nearly as much as he claims. Maybe I should have gone into the logging business instead of pourin' champagne. What do ya think?"

Ki answered, "His sons told us that they own this lake."

"Aw, horseshit!" Scotty snorted. "Which one said that?"

"Arnie, I think." Jessie looked at Ki. "I think he is the one whose shoulder you put out of commission."

Scotty blinked. "You hurt Arnie? Why, I don't see a mark on you. Seems downright impossible."

Ki just shrugged. Jessie said, "His brother Fred isn't feeling too good either. I'm afraid we were pretty rough on them this morning."

Scotty forced a laugh. "I get it, you're making a joke."

"It's not a joke," Ki said evenly. "They got rough with Jessie and they paid for it. We on their land, and they said they owned the lake."

"Well, they don't own a damn drop of water that comes from that lake, nor even the water where they dock their sidewheel steam ships. Like I said, most of what they log is free land that could be used by anyone. Trouble is, no one can stand up to the Yoders. A few have tried, and they all either got shot, or run off."

"We'll need a steamboat and a crew," Jessie said, her mind not conditioned to dwell on problems but rather to focus on the immediate and successful achievement of her objectives. Comstock miners were dying every day under Sun Mountain for lack of adequate timber. So she would not even consider the possibility of failure. "I want a steamer and an experienced crew. Is that possible, or will

68

they have to be brought up from San Francisco?"

"Hell, no, it ain't possible!" Scotty snorted. "There ain't anyone stupid enough to get out on the water knowing that the Yoder fleet will just sink them."

"First," Jessie said, "is there a vessel to be had? Anything that operates with steam."

"Sure, there are a few vessels around. Most of them are rotting at dockside. There used to be three or four logging companies that operated on the lake. But when the Yoders came in, they put them all out of business."

"Well," Jessie said, "we're going to see that logging is put back in business."

"I wish you'd decide on some other line of work, miss. Like I said, there ain't no law up here, and Clinton Yoder is as mean and dangerous as a teased snake. He'll strike when you least expect, and he'll shoot to kill."

"So we've been told," Jessie said. She forced a smile. "Scotty, we'd appreciate it if you'd tell us where we can find the owner of a steam vessel. Something big and strong enough to pull logs across the lake. I would also like to hire logging men not afraid to stand up to the Yoders."

"I'll pass the word around," Scotty promised. "As far as a steamer, there's a stern-wheeler at Crystal Cove, about three miles south of here. She is about eighty feet long, and the last I heard she still floats. Man who owns her is named Ken Bell, and I know the vessel was all set up to either haul lumber across the lake or pull big log floats to a sawmill."

"Do you think he'd help us get her into working order and then command the vessel?"

"I don't know. Ken has a wife and two children. Like I say, he's a good man, and he sure could use the money. But it'd be dangerous. Almost a sure way to get killed."

Ki said, "We would protect him."

69

"You will have enough trouble protecting yourselves," Scotty said. "How you gonna keep a man alive when he's standing out on the deck of a boat and someone ambushes him from the trees? Hell, samurai, there's nowhere to hide on that water!"

Ki said nothing as they left to visit Ken Bell and see about buying his stern-wheeler. There was a troubling element of truth to the old Forty-Niner's logic. *Te* was not going to be of much value if his enemies were separated by a couple of hundred feet of water.

Ken Bell was a big man in his forties who was missing his right leg. He repaired harnesses for a living. His beard was shot with silver, and there was a great deal of suffering around his eyes and no small amount of bitterness in his voice when he talked of his circumstances.

"So you want to buy the *Tahoe*," he said, gesturing toward the two-decker which looked to Jessie in bad need of work. "And you think that you can start logging up here."

Jessie nodded and tried to forestall the lecture she was certain would come. "We know about the Yoders. Scotty warned us what they would try to do. But we've already had our run-in with Arnie and Fred, and I don't believe either of them is anxious to try us again."

Jessie told the man what had happened, and he began to smile as he sat hunched down on a tree stump, working on a broken harness. "So you two got the better of the Yoders. Well, I'll be damned! Maybe I was wrong to underestimate you a minute ago. Maybe you can stand up to them for a while. But in the end, they'll either kill or break you. Clinton is too damned cagey and mean to let you get way with hurting his boys, and both Arnie and Fred are too proud not to try and get even."

70

Jessie told Ken Bell about the Comstock Lode and how the lack of timbering was killing miners. "I want to make a profit at this if I can," she admitted, "but that is secondary to the main purpose, which is to save lives and revitalize the Comstock."

"I know," Bell said. "Last year, that was sort of my idea too. You see, the Yoders know damn good and well that they hold the key to the timber situation up here. They're just waiting for the prices to climb a little higher. Then they'll sell in Nevada instead of in Sacramento. You have to understand that San Francisco and Sacramento are booming. California pays a pretty fine price for lumber. Both sides are always competing for the best lumber on this mountain. But the fact of the matter is the Yoders are holding back on their logging as the prices go higher. One of these days, they'll strip the shores a mile back from the lake all the way around."

The idea of that was truly appalling to Jessie, who said so.

"Yeah," Bell replied, "it would sure take the shine off this basin, all right. But it's bound to happen unless the Yoders are stopped. I tried to do it, and look what happened to me."

"You lost your leg because of the Yoders?" Jessie asked.

"I can't prove it, but I know it's true. They used an old buffalo rifle. One minute I was standing on deck, shouting orders to my men, the next I was in the water with my kneecap blown away. I damn near drowned, and then I damned near bled to death. If the water hadn't been so cold, I probably would have. So I'm lucky to be alive."

"Why don't you show me your vessel, and let's see if we can talk a price."

Bell shrugged. He laid his harness and needle down and said, "All right, Miss Starbuck. But I told ya what hap-

71

pened to me and what'll most likely happen to you and the samurai if you try logging on Lake Tahoe. I done what my conscience said I needed to do. From now on you've been warned, and I'll say no more about the dangers."

"Fair enough," Jessie told the man as he pushed himself up and used a single crutch under his right arm to move down toward the ship and the water.

"You know anything about vessels?" Bell asked as they reached the small jetty and prepared to board.

"Not much," Jessie admitted.

"Well, this one was used for a few years on the Sacramento River to haul freight. Like all the others, it was disassembled and then hauled up here on wagons and put back together again, bolt by bolt. She's only seventy feet long, so it's not in the same class as one you'd see working on the Mississippi or the Missouri. But she's got a good engine and boiler, and the paddles are almost new. The engine rotates the wheel about twenty times a minute. If you was trying to fight a strong upriver current, you'd not have the power to do anything more than haul a little tonnage. But here on the lake you could chain up a hundred logs and drag them across as easy as you please."

Jessie nodded. She and Ki walked from the stern to the bow. On the main deck there was the firebox and engine and boiler. The deck itself was not enclosed, and was badly in need of replacement, because it was here that most of the freight was stored. On the second deck, Jessie visited the wheelhouse, windowed on all four sides to give the pilot a 360-degree view. The decking on the top was in much better condition, though still was in need of repair. Because it took the brunt of the sun and hard weather, it was badly peeled and the wood was splitting.

"The hull," Ki said, "is it sound?"

"You bet it is," Bell said. "I've caulked it myself, and

there is barely a drop of water that leaks through."

Jessie studied the piles of chains and ropes. "I have to confess that Ki and I really will be needing some experienced help. We don't even know how to start the engine, though I suppose we could figure it out."

Bell scratched his head. He looked back toward the shore and his cabin. "My wife and kids are visiting family in Sacramento right now. They won't be coming back for a couple of weeks yet. If you decided to buy the *Tahoe* from me, I'd be willing to give you a little help."

"What is your asking price?"

"I got over six thousand dollars tied up in her. Course, now I realize that the way things are up here, I won't be able to sell her for that, but—"

"Six thousand dollars is fine," Jessie said, "providing you give us a trial run and teach Ki and me how to operate the vessel."

"You got a deal, Miss Starbuck!"

Jessie was pleased. "Why don't we find some help and go out right now."

Bell's grin faded. "It's a little late in the afternoon for that. The wind picks up pretty strong, and I'll need to find a couple of firebox tenders. Might be there's a couple of adjustments need to be made. Gauges to be checked and such."

Jessie was disappointed. However, the wind had picked up and there were whitecaps on the lake. "All right. You get some men to tend the fireboxes and we'll leave here promptly at eight o'clock tomorrow morning."

"It's a date," Bell said. "I just hope you know what you're doing when it comes to the Yoders. I'm afraid that you and Ki won't have much luck finding a regular crew in this neck of the woods. It's one thing to take a little run and stay down at this end of the lake; it'll be another to try

73

crossing the lake and bring back logs. You'll see the Yoder fleet and they'll see you. Might be trouble right away."

"I'll find sailors willing to fight if I have to go clear to the Barbary Coast to do it," Jessie vowed.

Bell didn't blink an eye as he said, "Miss Starbuck, I'm afraid that's about what you'll have to do. I'd help you, but I need the one leg I got left."

Jessie nodded. "Just take us out for a trial run tomorrow morning. If the vessel performs, you will have a draft for six thousand dollars in your hands by the end of the day."

Bell seemed almost euphoric at the prospect. "My wife thinks that this vessel is cursed. She blames it for all the things that have gone wrong between us over the past few years. You see, we once had saved a pretty good chunk of money, but every cent we owned and some we borrowed went to buy the *Tahoe* and have her shipped up here and reassembled. And then, after the accident . . . I just sort of went crazy for a while. I used to be a hell of a man, if you can believe it. Being one-legged has taken a lot out of me."

Ki said, "A man is a man because of his heart, not his legs. You showed courage. Maybe you should take the money and leave these mountains."

"Maybe I will," Bell said hopefully. "I've just had nothing but bad luck here. Two winters ago, we lost a baby to pneumonia. My wife hates these mountains. She says they're no good for us, and she wants to live in Sacramento, where it's warmer."

"Then do it," Jessie urged.

Bell looked out at the lake, which was full of waves. "I guess I will," he said. "A man can repair harnesses as good down below as he can up here. At the same time, he can keep warm doing it."

He forced a smile and said, "You folks go on back to Scotty's and rest up. I'll stay on board and start to working on things. There's nothing wrong with this vessel that a little paint and sanding wouldn't cure. She's a fine old lady, and she'll serve you well."

"Maybe I can find someone at Scotty's who will help us tomorrow morning," Jessie offered.

"All right. You just do that and then I won't have to worry about it and I can stay right here and work all night."

And that was how they decided to do it. Jessie and Ki disembarked and headed for their horses. Looking back down at the lake and the stern-wheeler, Jessie said, "We've got to find men, Ki. Men who not only can sail that thing and log timber, but men who can fight and have the steel in them to help us figure out how we can stand up against the Yoders and get timbering delivered to the Comstock."

"I don't think you'll find them here," Ki said.

"Then we'll leave for San Francisco as soon as possible," she decided. "The wharves and docks are filled with seamen who would jump at the chance to help for double wages."

Ki agreed. "Finding a captain for the vessel will be the hard part. Finding one that we can trust."

Jessie nodded. She could see Ken Bell hobbling around on the stern-wheeler. "I just hope that everything goes well tomorrow," she said. "I want that man to have his money and to leave in one piece."

"Maybe," Ki said thoughtfully, "I should stick around here tonight and sort of watch over him and the craft."

"Good idea," Jessie said. "But first, why don't you come on back to Scotty's so that we can get you some blankets and something to eat for your supper."

Because Ki did not want to leave Jessie unprotected, he agreed.

Chapter 8

Jessie finished her dinner and looked across the table at Scotty. "There's no point in delaying it," she told the man. "It sounds like your saloon is packed, and I'll find a few men who will be willing to go out on the lake with us tomorrow."

Scotty did not seem pleased. "You are sure stubborn, miss. But if your mind is set, then I'll go get their attention."

"Thank you."

Jessie stood up and followed Scotty into the saloon, where three of his employees were hard-pressed to keep the drinks coming fast enough to satisfy the rough and thirsty crowd.

Scotty crawled up on his own bar—something he would have killed anyone else for doing—and yelled, "All right everybody, listen up!"

The room quieted. Scotty continued. "I got a beautiful young woman here—"

Before he could say any more, hoots and cheers went up as men shouted for a woman. Scotty's cheeks flamed. "She's a lady, fer Crissakes! A rich lady who is fixin' to buy Ken Bell's stern-wheeler and do some logging. She wants to know if any of you boys are man enough to hire on with her."

The saloon fell into silence. Even though some of the men were drunk, they were still just sober enough to understand what Scotty was saying. Their smiles died, and most of them took a sudden interest in their feet.

Scotty's voice took on a hard edge. "You're about what I had figured," he said with derision.

Jessie pushed forward. Then, in order to be seen, she climbed up on a chair. She realized full well that insulting and humiliating these men would accomplish nothing. "Gentlemen," she said, "Scotty has been kind enough to allow me to speak for myself. It's true, I am looking for a couple of men to help on the *Tahoe* tomorrow morning. And if things go well and I buy the vessel, I'll want to hire an entire logging crew. My intentions are to log the shore of this lake, but do it selectively. The Comstock Lode is in desperate need of good timbering for its underground mines. My idea is to bring the logs into Crystal Cove and start a sawmill. But until that's operational, I'll send logs down a skid-road to the Carson River, where they'll be floated down to the sawmills east of Carson City."

A beefy teamster said, "You ever heard of the Yoder family and this crew, miss? They've got sixty, maybe seventy men."

"Yes," Jessie said in a defiant voice, "and I think it's high time that people up in this basin stood up to them and broke what amounts to a virtual monopoly. Don't you?"

"I'm just a teamster. That's all most any of us are," the man growled. "What you're trying to do is start a damned timber war and get a bunch of us killed."

Jessie dismissed the man and looked around the room. "I need two men to be at Crystal Bay in the morning. I'll pay them ten dollars each. Do I have any takers?"

Ten dollars was three or four days' wages, but she had no offers. Jessie's heart sank with disappointment. "All right," she said, hopping down from the chair and starting for her room, "think about it. If anyone changes their minds, be there in the morning."

As she was leaving, she heard Scotty say, "You men are always complaining there ain't no work nor money to be made in these mountains anymore. Well, you just let it walk outta this room. And tonight, goddammit, I ain't serving no free wine!"

Someone jeered and several more clapped their hands. But mostly, the crowd was subdued.

The two men left Scotty's Half Way House only minutes after Jessie departed the saloon. They slipped out quietly and rode out at a walk. When they reached a nearby meadow, they touched spurs and set their horses into a hard gallop. The cold night stars competed with a lemon wedge of moon to guide them north. They rode until midnight brought them to the edge of the Yoder timberland.

Carl Walters and Tip Henson rode up to the gate and helloed the massive rock fortress home of Clinton Yoder and his boys. There were still lights on, and the house looked like some medieval castle, for it had been constructed of heavy granite by Mexican rock-masons during the years when the Spanish ruled California. It was here that the rich Spanish Don Alfredo Merida had sent his large family up from the blistering heat of the central California valley to enjoy the cool mountain summers. The enormous rock fortress had been skilfully built to withstand Indian attacks and even the raging Sierra fires that swept through this country every fifty or sixty years. It was situated perfectly and was considered nearly impregnable, for it was strategically nestled on the end of a small peninsula, so that it was surrounded by water on three sides. The only way to ride into the fortress was straight on, and there were two guardhouses where Clinton Yoder kept a twenty-four-hour guard.

The guards stepped out of their little blockades with their rifles pressed to their shoulders. "Identify yourselves!"

"Walters and Henson!"

The guards relaxed. One said, "What the hell are you doing out at this time of night? Good way to get yourselves blowed out of the saddle."

Walters was the leader of the pair. "We got to talk to the boss," he explained. "We got to see him tonight."

"It better be important or he'll have your ass," the guard grumbled.

"It is important. Damned important."

"It's still your ass, not mine. Go on in. Arnie and Fred are still up. I think they got a couple of San Francisco women in there."

Tip Henson looked at his partner with growing apprehension. Henson wanted to get onto their payroll. He was not sure that this was a good idea, but since he had been at Scotty's he thought that he had no choice but to come along with Walters and make a good show of himself.

"You let me do the talking," Walters told the younger man. "We got to get to the old man and warn him about the *Tahoe* going out tomorrow. Our problem is that Arnie and Fred are not known for their hospitality. Especially this time of the night, when they're liquorin' it up with whores."

"Then maybe we ought to come back tomorrow," Henson said.

"It'll be too damn late."

They rode up to the house, and they could hear men's laughter, and then giggling from the whores. Dismounting, they tied their horses to a hitchrail and walked up to the house. Walters knocked loudly, and the voices inside fell silent for a minute until one of the brothers yelled, "Who the hell is it?"

"Carl Walters and Tip Henson. We need to see your pa."

The door swung open to reveal Arnie. His eyes were bloodshot, his hair mussed, and his shirt unbuttoned. Walters saw that he wore a large bandage on his shoulder. A skinny, bare-breasted girl with yellow hair was hanging onto his shoulder, and she looked anything but pleased about the intrusion. And in back of them, Fred and a chunky little brunette were passed out on the couch before the huge fireplace. "What the hell you want?" Arnie demanded.

Walters knew that he had no choice but to explain right now, although he would have preferred to speak to Clinton. "There's a woman staying at Scotty's. Her name is Starbuck, and she's talking about buying Ed Bell's sternwheeler and starting a logging operation out of Crystal Cove. We thought you and Mr. Yoder would like to know that they're lookin' for help."

Arnie blinked. He shook his head and stared, and it was clear his mind was fogged by liquor. "What'd you say the woman's name was?"

"Starbuck. The way I hear it, she is with a Chinaman and—"

"Well I'll be a sonofabitch!" Arnie hissed. "They weren't kiddin' when they said they were gonna do it."

Walters stepped inside with Tip close behind him. The room was enormous, with a rock fireplace that ran from floor to raftered ceiling. "I think we ought to tell your pa," he said.

"Shit!" Arnie cursed. "Pa ain't going to like this one damned bit." He turned and staggered away to get his father.

The yellow-haired girl gave Walters an angry look and then padded barefooted over to the couch. Without bothering to cover her small breasts, she slumped down beside the brunette. She took a thin Mexican cigarillo from the end table and stuffed it between a red slash of smeared lipstick. She lit the cigarillo and inhaled deeply.

"Couldn't you bastards have at least waited to tell 'em this until tomorrow morning?" she crabbed as smoke streamed out her nostrils.

Walters shook his head. Tip just stared, for he had not been much with women, especially yellowed-haired ones with such girlish figures and pert little breasts. Every whore that he had bought had been plump and big-breasted. He was thinking that small breasts were cute when old Clinton Yoder came stomping into the room, buckling on his trousers.

The lumber king was still impressive. His arms were no longer as big around as tree branches, but his great chest was massive and covered with a thick mat of white hair. His face had a ruined look and was dominated by a fist-busted nose and a massive jaw. He had a deep voice that was a growl, and it did not take a mindreader to see he was not pleased about being awakened.

Walters staggered backward as the old man reached out and grabbed him by the collar. Clinton Yoder balled up his fists and snarled, "You tell me exactly what the hell is going on down there and you leave nothing out. Understand me?"

Walters nodded. He fought down his own rising sense of panic, but even to himself his voice sounded so high-pitched as to be girlish. "Tip and I was at Scotty's a few hours ago. There's this Starbuck woman and this Chinaman and they're—"

Clinton's massive head swung around to regard his son. "Arnie, is that them?" he bellowed.

"It has to be, Pa."

Clinton released his grip on Walters and swung around. He stomped over to the couch, grabbed his other son up and slammed him back and forth until Fred awoke and at last began to struggle feebly. "Wake up, you drunken sot!" Clinton roared into his son's face.

It was a wonder that Fred's neck didn't snap. He came awake fast.

"What's wrong, what's the hell is wrong?" he mumbled, trying to focus.

Clinton lost all patience. He slapped Fred across the mouth, once, then once again, with the back of his hand. "You boys ain't worth catshit!" he hollered. "You boys are drinkin' and whorin' way too damn much these days!"

Fred mumbled something brokenly and Clinton shouted, "Get rid of these whores and clean yourselves up! You're gonna get that revenge you spoke of gettin' against the woman and the Chinaman. And you're gonna get it tomorrow when you sink that goddamn stern-wheeler!"

The yellow-haired girl grabbed her friend and practically dragged her from the room. Walters was wishing he could leave as well until old Clinton rumbled from deep in his chest, "You boys did right by coming here and telling us. You're gonna be a part of our little surprise. So pour yourselves a drink and tell me every damn thing you heard at Scotty's."

Walters nodded uneasily. He stared at Fred's mouth, which was bloodied, and he was thinking that this whole idea had been a mistake. But it was too late to turn things around now. He should have known that Clinton Yoder would not just issue a warning to Miss Starbuck. Most of all, he should have guessed that he and Tip were going to be a part of murdering the woman and the Chinaman.

Hell, Walters thought, *the Chinaman don't count, but I sure as hell hate to be a party to killing a pretty young woman.*

Morning dawned clear and cool, and Jessie was awake even before first light. She dressed, combed her hair, and went to see if she could talk the cook out of some coffee before he became too busy with breakfast. The cook was more than happy to oblige her, and Jessie took her coffee out on the porch of Scotty's and watched the sunrise flow across the alpine lake like liquid gold. The dark pines took shape and then were etched in with color. It was going to be a magnificent day. The water was absolutely calm.

"Good morning," Ki said, as he joined her. "Thinking about the *Tahoe* and our first trial run?"

"I've thought of little else since last evening," Jessie confessed. "I want that vessel to work for us and for the Comstock. Isn't it crazy sometimes how we start to do something and then our plans get changed in mid-stream— or, I guess in my case right now, mid-lake—and then suddenly we are off on another tangent?"

Ki nodded. "Everything is joined. No person can be unaffected by what others do."

Jessie sipped her coffee. "I know almost nothing about the logging business or about steamships, other than that my father designed the first iron-hulled ships to trade in the Orient."

"It is not important that you know about mechanical things, or about logging or mining," the samurai told her. "All that is necessary is that you know how to choose the right men who do understand such things. That is the most important."

"I was hoping that Ken Bell would stay and captain the ship. But he is leaving."

Ki said, "Mr. Bell has a wife and two daughters. He knows there could be much bloodshed before this is over."

"Yes." Jessie looked up at the samurai. "We need help, Ki, experienced loggers and seaman who know how to handle a steamship. We can't stand off the Yoders with prayers and good intentions. Not if they have sixty or seventy men and an entire fleet of vessels."

"I asked about that," Ki said. "It turns out that a 'fleet' means three large side-wheel steamers, Jessie. That is hardly the Royal Navy."

Jessie was surprised and relieved. "Only three?"

"Yes."

"Good. But I still think you should go to San Francisco at once and recruit us some men."

"I will do as you say, but it would be better for you to go while I stay here to guard the *Tahoe*."

Jessie considered that. "I guess you're right. From all I've heard, it would be in keeping with the Yoders to sabotage the vessel. But how could you possibly—"

"I will think of something even as I worry about you on the Barbary Coast. It is a very dangerous place, Jessie."

"I've been there before."

"But either your father or I have always been there with you."

"I'll be fine," Jessie said. "Why don't we have some breakfast? Since it doesn't appear that we'll have any help today, I guess that we'll both be shoveling wood into the firebox."

"Don't give up," Ki said. "Someone may show up to help yet."

85

                                    • • •

Eight o'clock proved the samurai correct. Two men, Carl
Walters and Tip Henson, were waiting beside the *Tahoe*
when Jessie and Ki arrived. After quick introductions,
Walters and Henson went right to work feeding the firebox
until the steam pressure had risen to an operating level.

Jessie and Ki joined Ken Bell in the wheelhouse on the
second deck. Bell blasted his steam whistle and reversed
the engine. Jessie felt a strong surge as the stern-wheeler's
paddles began to bite into the lake, churning up big, frothy
waves.

"It's the easiest thing in the world," Bell said with a
wide grin. "There's nothing finer than captaining a ship,
Miss Starbuck. Oh, a Mississippi riverboat captain would
say that this is pretty tame stuff. No reefs or sandbars or
shifting currents to worry about. The water level is always
deep and there are no hidden logs waiting to rip out your
hull. But when the wind picks up on Lake Tahoe and the
weather grows foul, it takes a lot of skill to avoid being
smashed into the rocks."

"I'm going to find someone who has that skill," Jessie
promised, as Bell again reversed his engine and swung the
wheel hard to port to set the vessel churning forward.

"I'll be honest with you, Miss Starbuck. This is going to
sound crazy, but if I were you I'd mount cannon on her.
Eight-pounders both port and starboard would even the
odds against the Yoders in a real hurry."

Jessie made a mental note to inquire about the cannon.
"Where are we going this morning?"

"The Yoder ships are working at the north end of the
lake right now, so we'll just stay down here at this end.
The lake is twenty-six miles long and almost half that
wide, so there sure isn't any reason for them to bother us.

Hell, Miss Starbuck, there's enough good timber along the shore to last a couple hundred years."

"Yes," Jessie said, "but the timber on the Nevada shore will be cheaper and easier to send over to the Comstock. And it seems to me that there are quite a few rocky bluffs where it would be hard to log."

"I'll give you this," Bell said, "you're observant. Yeah, a man like me or Clinton Yoder, or any experienced logging man for that matter, they can steam along the shore and pick out the best stands without ever setting a foot on shore. I'll point a few of them out to you. First one is right around that rocky point just ahead. It's where I was logging before when they ambushed me."

Jessie followed the man's eyes. The point was just a mile ahead, and the steamer was making good progress. Jessie had ridden a good many vessels like this, both on rivers and oceans. In both of those cases, the water was rough instead of still, and the *Tahoe* seemed to fly across the beautiful lake almost effortlessly.

They swept by the point and Bell pointed to a long, sandy beach. "That's called Hunter's Cove. See that stand of timber? It's prime, and it's close enough to shore so that it could damn near be rolled into the water. Get your logs trimmed and rope them together, then use the *Tahoe* to pull them to the skid-road."

"Just like that?"

Bell chuckled. "Nope. But I never promised you it would be easy. Still, it seems to me that you can't help but make a . . ."

Jessie saw the man's face change. "What's wrong?"

"We're losing power!"

Now Jessie felt it, and so did Ki.

Bell swung the stern-wheeler hard to starboard toward the beach. There were no rocks, and Jessie knew at once that the vessel's hull would not be damaged for her draft was less than two feet.

The captain shook his head. "I don't understand it! Ki, make sure that those two men are feeding the boilers. We've either got a leak or the fires are dying."

Ki jumped out of the wheelhouse and ran to the steps leading down to the first deck. He ducked down the stairs just in time to see both Walters and Henson take a running jump over the side of the *Tahoe*. They landed with a tremendous splash in the chilling water, and though both men were obviously poor swimmers, they tried to swim madly for the rocky point.

Icy fear mixed with frozen dread swept though the samurai. There was only one explanation why two men would abandon ship in such a desperate manner. The samurai went flying down the stairs, knowing that dynamite was set to blow the ship to pieces. Ki struck the lower deck on the run. There was seventy feet of deck to cover, and he knew that he had to get lucky to have any chance at all.

He did get lucky. The two men had been overanxious to jump ship and had hid the bundle of dynamite without much ingenuity. Ki saw a thin cloud of white smoke and he scooped up the dynamite on the run. The fuse was less than an inch from the point of explosion when the samurai's arm cocked back over his shoulder and then shot forward.

"You forgot something!" he shouted, throwing the large bundle of dynamite as far as he could after the two thrashing swimmers.

Both of the men in the water stopped as the sound of his voice carried loudly across the water's surface. Then, as the bundle reached the apex of its looping arc and began to drop, they screamed and began to thrash wildly.

The dynamite exploded just before it struck the lake's placid surface. There was a thunderous roar and a blossom of white smoke. A towering pillar of water lifted upward. The shock and blast knocked the samurai over. The *Tahoe* rocked violently as the sound of the explosion boomed across the water to strike the mountainsides and echo back and forth across the lake.

Ki rose unsteadily to his feet just as the *Tahoe*'s hull struck the sandy beach. The ship lurched violently, and as the samurai was hurled into a stanchion he heard the sound of timber ripping down below.

For a moment Ki was knocked unconscious. When his mind cleared, Jessie was at his side. "Are you all right?" she asked worriedly.

Ki touched the side of his head and felt a large goose-egg. "I've felt better," he said, struggling to his feet.

Ken Bell looked sick. He was leaning over the side of the *Tahoe* and when he could see nothing, he ran to a hatch and disappeared. He was back a moment later, wet up to his waist. "The hull is ruptured and we're sinking to the sand. I don't know what happened or how bad the damage is because it's totally dark in there. But it's obvious we're finished."

"Why?" Jessie demanded. "Maybe the damage is only minor."

Bell shook his head and said in a downcast voice, "I wish I could believe that. But the water is coming in too fast."

Ki stripped off his vest and collarless tunic, then finally his sandals. "I'll go down and take a look," he said. "We have to know."

Without waiting for comment, the samurai dove into the clean, cold water and swam down to inspect the damaged hull of the *Tahoe*. It was still not quite clear what had happened, but Ki suspected that the explosion had sent such a shock force through the water that the hull had ruptured very badly. And now, as he inspected the damaged hull of the stern-wheeler, his worst fears were being confirmed. Being a shallow-bottomed vessel, there was much of her underside that was resting on sand and impossible to inspect. But what was visible and had been facing the port side which had taken the force of the shock looked bad. The hull was ruptured so severely that Ki could see splits in the wood that ran twenty and thirty feet long. If it were not for the fact that the vessel was beached, it would have sunk in minutes.

Ki shot back up to the surface. The water was numbingly cold, and Ken Bell dropped a rope ladder. The samurai climbed it with ease, his long, supple muscles rippling with the effort.

"How bad is it?" Bell asked.

"I'm afraid it's split. The underside of the ship looks like the bark of a tree that has been ripped by a grizzly bear's claws."

Ken swore softly to himself. "Then I'm ruined," he said, fists clenched to his side. "Everything I ever owned is tied up in this ship, and now it's lost."

Jessie came to the man's side. "If you'll stay here and help, maybe you and Ki can repair the hull while I'm in San Francisco."

Ed looked up. "How can we do that?" he asked. "She's got to be dry-docked for us to work on her undersides. It would take a train locomotive to pull her up on this beach."

Jessie thought about that for a minute. "Unfortunately, there isn't a train available. But every night at Scotty's Half Way House there are no less than a dozen freighters stopping. If we could hire them and their teams, maybe they could do it."

"Uh-uh," Bell said dejectedly. "They've got mule

teams, horse teams, and oxen. They'd never hitch 'em all up together."

"They would," Jessie said, "if Scotty threatened to raise his rates and cut off their free wine. They'd do it in a minute if I also offered a hundred dollars to every team that joined up and tried."

"It would take fifty teams."

"Then we'll advertise it for a couple of weeks!" Jessie said, not giving a damn if it cost her ten thousand or fifty thousand dollars to get this ship back on the water and operating with cannon fixed to her decking. "If we can get it up on dry-dock, are you willing to stay and help fix it?"

Ken Bell stuffed his big hands into his pockets. He looked his vessel over. Maybe he was thinking about how he had once scraped, painted, or polished every square foot of her. "Miss Starbuck," he said finally, "you promised me six thousand dollars for the *Tahoe,* and I promised to turn her over to you in good, serviceable condition. Mechanically, I've proved her worth already."

"Yes, you have," Jessie said.

"Then I'll see to it that the hull is repaired better than ever. We've got the timber all around us. We'll saw it, plane it, and then fit it to the hull. And when that's done, we'll load the decks with lumber and sail across this lake with our whistles blasting right in the Yoder people's faces!"

Jessie extended her hand. "It's a deal," she said. "If we don't give up, we'll never get beat."

"Only dead," Bell said quietly as, far out on the lake, a Yoder ship began to blast its steam whistle. The distant noise sounded like mocking laughter.

Chapter 9

The word had spread very quickly. All along the Sierra passes freighters and teamsters argued back and forth about the one-hundred-dollars-a-team payment and the possible repercussions of opposing Clinton Yoder and his huge army of loggers. At first, few men were inclined to take Jessie's cash offer seriously. But then a lawyer from San Francisco told everyone that Miss Jessica Starbuck was one of the richest and most powerful women in the world. After that, the skeptics were hooted at and people began to take Jessie's offer very seriously. And the first thing anyone knew, Scotty's Half Way House was jammed with teamsters, newspaper reporters, and curiosity seekers. When the inn itself was filled, people slept in blankets out under the pines. On the anticipated day, there were more than five hundred people heading for the beached sternwheeler at Hunter's Cove.

"Hell," Scotty said, "with this many folks, we don't even need the freighters to hitch their teams up. We can do it with manpower!"

Jessie laughed. She had a roll of one-hundred-dollar bills in her coat pocket, and she was driving a wagon loaded with heavy rope. There did not seem to be any doubt in her mind that the *Tahoe* could be dry-docked with this much help.

The crowd was jovial and excited. Everybody knew that the Yoders might try something, and so they were also well armed. There was rough talk, talk of lynching the damned Yoders and their men if they tried to intervene.

"Do you really believe the old devil will come?" Jessie asked Scotty, who rode beside her on the buckboard.

"You mean Clinton?"

"Yes, and his sons."

Scotty scratched his stubbly beard. "I can tell you this much. Clinton Yoder is like a longhorn bull. You wave a red blanket in front of him, he'll lower his head and come in hooking his horns."

"So you think he'll come."

Scotty patted the gun on his hip. "I'd be right surprised if he isn't there already."

That prediction caused Jessie a great deal of concern. Ki was guarding the *Tahoe*, but even the samurai was no match for the Yoders and their entire crew. Still, yesterday there had been at least two hundred armed freighters and spectators camped at Hunter's Cove, and Jessie could not imagine the Yoders being insane enough to attack all those people.

"I wish we could hurry along a little faster," Jessie said.

"Five minutes one way or the other won't change what's going to happen, Miss Starbuck."

Jessie didn't agree. Five minutes of indecision or delay had caused entire armies to win or lose their battles. Five minutes could and had changed the course of history.

She was still thinking that when they finally rounded the point and saw the three big sidewheel steamers floating about a quarter of a mile off the beach. Jessie's heart skipped a beat and she said, "Why didn't you tell me they had cannons?"

"Because they never did before," Scotty said in a thick voice.

The crowd following them also fell silent, and it was clear that the same thought was on their minds. Rifles against rifles or pistols against pistols? Sure! They were more than a match for old Clinton Yoder and his men. But they had no chance at all against cannons.

He wouldn't dare, Jessie told herself.

"Look!" someone yelled. "They're lowering a dinghy!"

Jessie said, "Put the whip to this team, Scotty. I got a feeling that I am finally about to meet with Clinton Yoder."

She was right. The huge man with the white beard wore a slouched black hat whose brim drooped down over the back of his neck as well as over his forehead. Jessie watched as Clinton climbed down a rope ladder into the boat. His two sons, also large and broad-shouldered, could be seen in command of separate vessels. They were standing next to the cannons, which were obviously primed and ready to be fired.

"He's holding the winning hand," Scotty muttered. "Three of a kind."

"We'll see," Jessie said, her eyes going over the decks of the *Tahoe* where she saw Ki waiting with his arms folded over his chest in a defiant posture. But defiant or not, Jessie knew she could not risk a naval confrontation. Not against the three big cannons that were now pointed right at the *Tahoe*. The poor stern-wheeler, lying on the shore with her stem out of the water and her stern down low and half submerged, appeared to be as pathetic and vulnerable as a beached whale.

When Jessie reached Hunter's Cove, she was besieged by the crowd, who wanted to know what was going to happen. One freighter pretty well summed up the general sentiment when he said, "It ain't worth no hundred dollars for me to get my oxen blowed all to hell by them cannons, ma'am."

"He won't do that," Jessie said. "That's why he's coming to talk."

Jessie joined Ki and Ken Bell on the beach as the crowd gathered all around them and watched as Clinton Yoder was rowed in closer to the shore. All conversation stopped, and the only thing that could be heard was the rhythmic dipping of the oars and the gentle splashing of the water against the *Tahoe*'s damaged hull.

"That's far enough!" Clinton roared when his boat was within fifty feet of the shore. He stood up and faced the huge crowd, his eyes dark with rage. "Miss Starbuck!"

Jessie stepped right to the edge of the water. "What do you want here?" she demanded.

"This lake and its surrounding timber is under my domain. I came first and I claim it for my own."

"It's *not* yours, None of it except perhaps where your home and sawmill are situated belongs to you," Jessie said. "I intend to repair the hull of this vessel and log timber off this lake. There's enough for both of us."

"Is there?" Clinton shouted. "And if I did allow you to operate on this lake, how would I stop others? Where would I draw the line?"

"It's not your decision one way or the other," Jessie said. "You have no right."

Even from a distance, Jessie saw how the old timber king's face grew red with suffused blood. "By damn," he screamed, "I will stop you and anyone else that tries to float that vessel or any other!"

Jessie turned to face the crowd. "You've just heard the challenge. There's rope in the buckboard, and you can all

96

see the rolling logs cut and ready for the weight of the *Tahoe*. Hitch your teams and prepare to earn a hundred dollars. This man has no legal right to stop this."

But Clinton wasn't finished. "If you pull that vessel up on the beach, I swear that I'll blow it—and you—all to hell!"

Jessie took a deep breath. When no one moved, she walked over to the buckboard and hauled off a section of heavy line. Ki, Scotty, and Ken Bell were right beside her, and together they pulled off the rope. Ken and Ki carried two lengths of it up onto the deck of the *Tahoe* and secured both lines to stanchions.

"Doesn't anyone here have the courage to help?" Jessie shouted. "Are you all willing to concede this lake to a single man who has no claim on it? You men ought to be ashamed of yourselves!"

A heavyset teamster separated himself from the others and plodded forward through the sand. "I'll take that line," he hissed, glaring at Clinton Yoder. A moment later, he had a span of oxen backing toward shore. He tied the line to a singletree and then he stood back, legs spread apart, with a whip in his hand. *"Yahhh!"* he shouted, snapping the whip.

The huge oxen dug their cloven hooves into the sand and strained into the harness. They were so powerful that the *Tahoe* actually slid forward almost five feet, but the higher it came out of the water, the more difficult it was to pull, and the vessel was soon stuck.

The other teamsters fidgeted. Then, when one of the mighty oxen bawled and fell to its knees, something seemed to take hold of the crowd, and all at once everyone was moving, grabbing more line from the buckboard,

97

backing their teams down the beach, and hitching up to pull.

Jessie felt tears of gratitude burn her eyes. She watched as Ken Bell and Ki worked furiously to fasten lines and chains to the deck. Powerful draft horses stamped nervously. Mules, solid and secure, stood patiently while more oxen with massive shoulders were readied.

Jessie hopped up into the back of the buckboard. So many men were yelling all at once that she drew her six-gun from her holster and raised it overhead. She fired once, and the noise died as her shot echoed back and forth across the great Sierra basin. "All right!" she told them. "At the second shot, let's all pull together and get this vessel out of the water!"

The men roared with approval. Clinton Yoder and his three sidewheel steamers with their cannon were forgotten, or at least ignored. Jessie twisted around to see Yoder being rowed furiously back towards his ship. She turned back toward the trees and fired her six-gun.

Oxen threw their massive bulks into their harnesses. Horses and mules did the same, and hundreds of men grabbed the lines and pulled until the chords in their necks stood out like stretched wires. The seventy-foot-long sternwheeler seemed to groan as its tremendous weight was lifted up onto the rolling logs. Then it began to come out of the lake, slowly at first, as the logs closest to the water were buried by the massive and concentrated weight of the vessel, then faster as the weight was distributed over more logs which began to roll upward.

Jessie had never seen anything to equal the Herculean effort that she now witnessed. Hundreds of men and animals groaned and strained until, finally, the *Tahoe* made a sucking sound as it was jerked completely out of the wet sand. The stern-wheeler's paddles caught up for a moment, and the vessel's momentum almost shifted backward, but the paddles began to turn again as men and beasts gave it everything they had in one last desperate effort.

"Tie the lines to the trees!" Ken Bell shouted. "Secure the lines!"

It was done in a moment. The lines were secured to the trees and the ship was dry-docked a good ten feet above the shoreline.

Jessie threw her hands up in the air in victory.

But out on Lake Tahoe, Clinton Yoder, now back on the deck of his ship and in command, threw his arm down in a slashing motion. His big cannon belched smoke and fire. A massive cannonball screamed across the water to smash the beached stern-wheeler's paddles to kindling wood.

Jessie looked up at Ki and Ken Bell atop the vessel. "Jump!" she cried.

They both jumped. The entire beach with its men and animals went crazy with panic as the other two Yoder steamships opened fire. Jessie hit the sand as the stern of the *Tahoe* disintegrated in a shower of timber. Animals went crazy and broke their harnesses, men were knocked to the beach and trampled by the teams and by the crowd, which went scrambling up the beach for the cover of the pine trees.

But it was over even before the echoes died across the mountains. The *Tahoe* lay wrecked, its stern a smoldering mass of fire and splintered timbering. And out on the lake, the three sidewheelers began to blast their steam whistles. Their crews were shouting and jeering as their ships turned and steamed north.

Jessie lay stunned in the sand. The huge crowd seemed

frozen by shock, and yet not one man had been killed, not one animal seriously injured.

But the *Tahoe* was destroyed, and Jessie knew that this first and decisive battle was lost. She was going to San Francisco to find a naval officer who could fight cannon with cannon. It was her only hope.

Chapter 10

Jessie caught a ride with a freighting man that Scotty recommended as a personal friend. She ticketed the Central Pacific Railroad at Norden and rode it to Sacramento, where she boarded a steam packet and completed the final leg of her journey to San Francisco. On Market Street, she met with several of her business associates, men she trusted and who had been trusted by her father.

"The Comstock Lode is being strangled," she told the executives. "In all truthfulness, the Comstock may be said to be the tomb of the forests of the Sierras. Millions on millions of feet of lumber are buried there, lumber which will never again see the light of day. I have been told by reliable sources that no less than eighty million feet of timber is consumed annually."

Jessie paused so that the enormity of the figures could be digested. "I have seen the eastern slopes of the Sierras and, gentleman, they are completely denuded for a distance of almost sixty miles. Logging operations are now working far below the Walker to the south and the Truckee to the north of Reno. The logging has spilled over into the Tahoe Basin, one of the last good timber reserves to be had within fifty miles. And even it would have been logged out by now if it were not for the fact that logs must be floated across the lake and then conveyed over the rim of the

Sierras before they can be skidded down to the Carson Valley. That, and the fact that a man named Clinton Yoder has a virtual stranglehold on the basin."

The San Francisco executives were spellbound. Mining stock on the lode was doubling almost annually and had done so for a good number of years. After the California Gold Rush, San Francisco had withered like an old flower only to be resurrected again, bigger and better than ever because of Comstock gold and silver. The idea of the Comstock being strangled by the lack of timber caused these men to tremble. The realization that a single family could actually monopolize the Tahoe timber was outrageous.

"Surely we can deal with the man, Miss Starbuck," one of them said. "Buy him out, preferably; but if not, compete successfully. We can carry the loss for years if that's what is necessary to get good timber to the Comstock. No price is too great."

Jessie smiled. "How about a timber war?"

They gaped at her. Jessie went on to relate how the Yoders and their side-wheel steamers had used cannon to destroy the *Tahoe* after they had dry-docked it at Hunter's Cove.

"My God!" Mr. Anson Thaber said. "How in the world can a man get away with such a thing?"

"With a small army," Jessie stated flatly. "He probably pays his men top dollar, and he hires only those who will fight for him. If he had killed anyone, we would have gone after them and the devil take the consequences. But as it happened, he was careful and his aim was very good. He simply managed to destroy our vessel's paddlewheel and stern."

"Can it be repaired?"

"Yes," Jessie said, "although there is no guarantee that

it won't be attacked by cannon again and again."

"Then what is the answer?"

"I'm not sure," Jessie admitted. "I need to find a captain who has logged up in the Pacific Northwest. One who understands what we are up against and is willing to fight."

"But how," exclaimed a man named Percy, "could you possibly expect any one man to stand up against so many ships and sailors?"

"I don't," Jessie said. "I expect one man to command a crew of hard men who are willing to take great risks in order to win great rewards. I want men who are loggers, yes. But even more, I want sailors who are willing to fight!"

"It sounds to me like you want a bunch of pirates," Percy said.

Jessie smiled. "If their captain understands anything about logging, then yes, pirates would do fine."

The gentlemen shook their heads in silent disapproval.

"You are taking too great a risk, Miss Starbuck," big George Arnold said. "Far too great a risk."

"My father built a business empire that spans the globe," Jessie reminded them. "And he did it primarily because he wasn't afraid of taking necessary risks. Miners are dying every day up on the Comstock. *They* take risks! They take them because they have families to feed. Well, I take this risk because I'd never forgive myself if I walked away and did nothing, if I let one man stand in the way of progress and be the cause of hundreds of needless deaths each year."

Jessie stood up. Her eyes moved up and down the long executive table. The average age of the men she faced was probably sixty, and they had all proven themselves extremely able, if not brilliant, administrators and managers. "My father respected this body. He often consulted with you and sought your opinion just as I am doing now."

Percy cleared his throat. "It's our opinion that the authorities ought to be involved. Lake Tahoe is not this man's private domain. Let the authorities handle it."

Jessie raised her chin. "The authorities, meaning the state bureaucrats and politicians? Yes," she said, "I suppose they could get an injunction against the Yoder family and eventually make them cease their logging and close their sawmill. But that would take years, and too many lives will have been lost. No, this requires immediate action. Can any of you recommend someone with the qualifications I seek?"

The men down the long polished oak table stared at their hands, or the ceiling and remained silent.

Jessie turned to leave. "Don't panic and sell your mining stock just yet, gentlemen. I intend to win this fight. To do that, I intend to find a pirate captain and a pirate crew. I will pay enough money to buy cannons and whatever it takes to win."

"What about a ship?" Thaber asked. "Won't you have to have a new ship? And won't it take at least a year to disassemble one, haul it by boat, then railroad, and finally by packtrain to Lake Tahoe?"

Jessie took a deep breath. "I don't know," she said. "Ki and the man I bought the *Tahoe* from are trying to rebuild it right now. The paddlewheel and the paddles can be made easily enough. But there's the ripped hull. When I left, it did not look very optimistic. But I know that my samurai will not quit. I know that he'll refuse to be defeated, and will not only rebuild the *Tahoe,* but have it ready and waiting to sail when I return with help."

"There must be some way we can help you," a man said.

"I think you already have." Jessie smiled at them.

"You've told me I need a pirate, maybe an entire crew of them. Perhaps you're right. I shall find such a man."

They were astonished and, from their expressions, obviously troubled. They were staid, conservative men. Good, law-abiding men, respected civic leaders. Among the entire lot of them, not one knew the name of a single pirate—retired or active.

Jessie left them. She went down to a seedy used-clothing store on the wharf and bought a cheap dress and some fake jewelry and black stockings. You didn't go into the Barbary Coast district looking as if you had money. And you didn't go without carrying a gun and a knife.

Jessie returned to her hotel and changed into the used clothes. They smelled of cheap perfume and bad whiskey, and they were stained and wrinkled. She put them on with distaste and slipped a derringer into a garter that fit snugly around her thigh. She slipped the knife down inside her bodice. Either way, if some man grabbed for the goodies, she was going to present him with some hard, cold steel.

It was early evening on the San Francisco waterfront, and Jessie was looking for a man to escort her from saloon to saloon while she hunted her pirate captain. He didn't really have to be a pirate in the truest sense of the word, but he did have to enjoy a good fight, even against long odds. He had to be an adventurer and something of a rogue. *Maverick* was the term used for such a man in Texas.

"Hey, honey," a drunken sailor called, "how much for a poke in the alley?"

Jessie ignored him and hurried on until she saw another man watching her closely. He was quite young and not a bit bold. There were pimples on his unshaven cheeks, but he was tall and had a nice face. Jessie went straight to him and he almost fell over.

"Hi," she whispered, "buy me a drink?"

The young man looked over his shoulder to make certain that it was he that she was addressing. "Why, sure," he said, excitement rising in his voice, making it high and nervous. "Why, hell, yes, lady! My name is Billy Sawyer."

"Mine is Jessie," she said, taking his arm. Billy would do to get her in and out of the waterfront dives. If bigger, stronger men challenged him for her company, Jessie knew that she might have a problem, but she would face that when and if it occurred.

"How about this one?" she asked.

Billy looked plenty worried. "Pretty rough in there."

"I can take care of myself," Jessie said, wishing with all her heart that it was Ki whose arm she was clinging to.

"All right, then," the young sailor said, filling his chest and raising his chin. "Let's have a drink and get acquainted."

Jessie smiled and Billy squeezed her hand. His palms were sweaty and she wished that he would just let go of her and relax while she surveyed the men and searched for someone who seemed to have the look of a rogue and a fighter.

The moment she stepped inside the saloon, all conversation stopped and Jessie realized that she was definitely going to have a problem. So did the young sailor. He seemed to shrink at the crude catcalls and the obscenities that were directed at Jessie.

"Ignore them," Jessie said as she practically pulled Billy to a nearby table where the light was poorest and she would not be clearly observed. "Just pretend we're alone."

"I wish we *were* alone," Billy said. "I could get us a bottle and we could go and—"

"No," Jessie said, cutting him off short. "I just want some company for a while. That's all."

106

"You mean . . ."

Jessie slipped a twenty-dollar bill under the table. It took Billy so completely by surprise that he stammered, "But *I'm* the one that supposed to buy *you* drinks!"

"Let's play the game differently this evening," Jessie said. "I'll buy the drinks and you just do as I say and get me out of here when I'm ready to leave. Is that clear?"

"I . . . why, I guess so," he said, looking both hurt and confused. "What kind of woman are you, anyway?"

Jessie reached over and squeezed his hand. "The kind you aren't interested in knowing," she told him.

"Well, you sure are beautiful," he said. "You're the prettiest woman I ever sat with before."

Jessie sighed. She hadn't wanted a foul-mouth mauler, but neither had she wanted a puppy like this. He was so obviously a cabin-boy out of his natural element.

He ordered rye whiskey, and Jessie took a glass of cognac. They were quiet, aware that many eyes were upon them. Jessie only half listened as Billy Sawyer told her about his ship, the *Wayward Horn*. He actually was a cabin boy, though he never used the word, and tried to impress her otherwise. He had been to England once, and to the coast of North Africa.

"It is a world you cannot imagine," he said with a faraway look in his eyes. "There are men who would cut your throat for pleasure. They say that this Barbary Coast is rough and murderous. But's really not. I've been to hell and back, Jessica. And I know how to take care of a woman like you."

Jessie could not help but smile with amusement. The young man mistook her smile for something more promising, and when he tried to slip his arm around her waist, Jessie drove her elbow into his ribs so hard he spilled his rye and began to cough.

107

"What'd you do that for?"

"Because I don't like for men or boys to take their liberties with me unless it's my choice," she told him, studying the men at the bar and wondering if any of them might be her man. "Billy, I'm looking for a sea captain with logging experience. Would you know of such a man?"

His pride had been grievously injured. He pouted and would not speak. Jessie scowled. She raised her hand and ordered him another drink, and only then did he speak. "I do know such a man."

"What is his name?"

"Griff Hastings. But he's not a captain. At least, not anymore. He's the first mate on my ship. He knows everything about logging and shipbuilding, for his father was a logging man and he taught Griff everything."

"Has he ever been a pirate?"

"A pirate?"

"Yes."

Billy shook his head. "Naw, Griff is a fine man. His only problem is that he is too quick to fight. But in all things of the sea and ships, he is the best. Tough, too. More than once I've seen him clear out a saloon even rougher than this one all by himself."

"It sounds as if you admire him greatly."

Billy shrugged. "I admire no man . . . well, except my pa, who died last year. He was a bosun's mate. Said I'd be one too. And maybe I will. I don't know. The sailing life is hard, but it's good for a man."

"I'm sure it is," Jessie said. "But back to this Griff Hastings fellow. Can he be trusted? Is he a loyal friend?"

"Sure he is. He's either your best friend or your very worst enemy. There is nothing in-between for Griff Hastings."

"Perfect!" Jessie said. "He sounds just perfect. I must see him at once."

"But what do you need him for?"

"I want to hire him to operate my stern-wheel steamer up on Lake Tahoe," Jessie said, deciding there was no reason for not being candid. "I am not what you think, despite these clothes."

"You own a steamship?"

"Yes," Jessie said. "Actually, I own a fleet of steamships. Have you ever heard of the Starbuck Lines?"

"Well, sure!"

"My name is Jessica Starbuck. I inherited that line from my father, Alex Starbuck."

He gaped at her. "I don't believe it!"

Jessie reached under the table and pulled out her derringer. "This was my father's gun. Look at his initials: A. S. And see the Lone Star insignia? It's the very same one that you see on all of my ships. I'm sure you recognize it."

Billy was very impressed. "That derringer is silver-plated, and the insignia is gold."

"Yes. But the gun still works fine," Jessie said, removing it from sight. There were two large men watching her very closely now. She could feel their lascivious stares as they mentally stripped her.

"Do you believe me now?"

Billy nodded.

"Will you take me to this first mate of yours so that we can speak in private?"

"But what about us?"

Jessie knew it was time to salvage his wounded pride. "I'd like nothing better than to spend more time with you. But I can't. I have men in danger and I need your help. If you would introduce me to this Griff Hastings, then I will pay you well."

"There isn't enough money to pay me so that I could find a woman as beautiful as you," he said.

"Then I'll pay you enough money to have several women, if that is your wish tonight."

He blushed. "I can't believe that—"

They were interrupted by two sailors. One of them, the larger of the two, slammed his bottle down on their table and leered at Jessie. "Come drink with men," he ordered.

Billy Sawyer started to protest, but the second man grabbed Billy's glass of rye whiskey and hurled it into his face. As Billy choked and sputtered, the man drew back his fist and punched him. The cabin boy cried out and went over backward in his chair, his nose broken and blood gushing over his lips and chin.

Jessie used that moment's distraction to draw her two-shot derringer. As the first man reached for her, she pointed it at his face and whispered, "Freeze or I'll put a ball through your brain!"

But the man was a fool. He tried to rip the derringer from her fist. Jessie shot him right between the eyes. His hand fluttered up to his face; then, with an expression of complete surprise, he crashed over the table and was dead.

Suddenly, the room exploded in violence as men began to draw their weapons and open fire. Jessie tried to shoot the second man, who lunged for her, but he managed to knock her arm upward. Then he slammed his shoulder into her and they rolled to the floor as more gunfire erupted. The lights went out. A man screamed in agony. Jessie felt powerful fingers groping for her throat. She bit the hand and screamed, "Billy, get Hastings! Quick!"

The man on top of her seemed to have eyes in the dark. He found her throat again and began to throttle the life out of her. Jessie fumbled for her knife, but he tore her hand away from her bosom and plunged his own clawing fingers down the front of her dress. Jessie raked him with her fingernails and he bellowed in pain, then lashed out with a brutal swing that connected on the side of Jessie's head.

She felt herself being choked to death and realized that she had no chance if she struggled. She was like a bird caught in the talons of an eagle. She went limp. Then, miraculously, the man's choking fingers relaxed. He picked her up in the swirling chaos and threw her over his shoulder. Then he smashed through the crowd and staggered into the street.

Jessie heard running footsteps. Then the man who carried her yelled to someone else, "To the ship before someone sees us! This woman is Jessica Starbuck! She's richer than a goddamn Egyptian pharaoh!"

Jessie tried to throw her weight violently to one side and bring the powerful man down. Instead, he dropped her right onto the paving stones so hard that the air was knocked from her lungs. Then he knelt down over her and shoved a gag into her mouth and tied it with a filthy bandanna. "Eli Green is dead," he said to his companion. "She shot him right between the goddamn eyes. She's slippery as an eel and twice as dangerous."

He threw Jessie back over his shoulder. "Let's go!"

Jessie tried to struggle, but she was helpless. She wanted to call for Ki to help save her. Only this time he was hundreds of miles away. She was lost. There was only one slim hope, and that was with a stranger named Griff Hastings. A man who cleaned out saloons all by himself.

Maybe Billy would help. But then again, Billy was weak. And she could hear gunfire exploding in the saloon. It would not surprise her even a little if Billy Sawyer were already dead.

Chapter 11

Griff Hastings lay in his berth aboard the Wayward Horn as he painstakingly carved a small duck out of teakwood. His hands were thick and heavy with calluses, but his long fingers were sensitive. He was good at carving waterfowl, having learned in China how to sculpt them with grace and a certain delicate turn to their outstretched wings. The deck around his berth was littered with wood chips, but he would clean up before he blew out the candle and slept. Griff was a tall, broad-shouldered man with sandy hair and serene gray eyes that were at odds with the scar tissue in his brows. His nose was bent, yet that somehow added to rather than detracted from his appearance. His lips were thin and he was clean shaven, with a heavy jaw and wide mouth.

For reasons he had never understood, Griff magnetized women. Short, tall, pretty, plump—of any race or nationality. If Griff had ever bothered to ask them what in the world they found appealing in a common looking man like himself, they would have said that he was somehow dangerous and exciting without being crude or rough. Contradictions, perhaps; but then, Griff was a contradiction himself. The son of a wealthy timber merchant from Seattle, he had eschewed taking over his father's business to take up a common sailor's life. From the age of fifteen he had been on every imaginable kind of ship, from whalers to gunships outfitted to hunt pirates. Griff had enjoyed every voyage, the rougher the better—up until the last one, when a certain Captain Samuelson had ordered him bound hand and foot to the forward mast to receive sixty lashes he did not deserve. Captain Samuelson had not appreciated Griff's leadership or seamanship, both of which characteristics Samuelson himself sadly lacked.

Griff had taken the lashes without struggle or protest because he had given many himself; and a captain's orders, even though unfair or even malicious, were always to be followed to the letter. But the captain had administered the lashes personally, which was unheard of. And not only that; once Griff had been securely bound to the mast the captain had replaced the normal cat-o'-nine-tails with a whip that had bits of whalebone woven into its lash. The whalebone ripped open flesh like the claws of a tiger. The captain had used every ounce of his considerable strength to open up Griff's back and reach the kidneys and vital organs. In a rage of frenzy and curses, the insecure bastard had almost killed his innocent and loyal first mate. Almost as damaging, he had nearly destroyed Griff's spirit, which had been his main intention.

All during the agony of his unjust punishment, Griff had refused to cry out or beg for mercy. He had bit the tip of his tongue off, and did not even whimper until he lost consciousness, the last ten blows. For days he had been delirious with pain while his shipmates nursed him and managed to keep him alive. When the voyage was ended and they were just two men once more and equals, Griff had relentlessly stalked Samuelson across Europe and then across the Mediterranean Sea to Tripoli in North Africa. Samuelson had broken in his terror and had ended his life with a hangman's noose of his own making.

Griff had cursed the strangled figure who had robbed him by bare minutes of revenge. He had called him a rabbit caught in a noose, and had screamed, "Why? Why, damn you?" at the dangling figure with its protruding tongue and bloated blue face. But the tormented eyes had only stared at him. There had been no answer. And so the first mate had set the room on fire and burned down an entire hotel. Miraculously, no one else died that afternoon.

But after that, rumors spread that Griff had tormented and then torched the captain while the man yet lived. It had been two years before any other captain had dared to sign Griff on for a voyage. During that time, the first mate had worked for his father's logging operation. But he was a sailor first, and he loved the sea most of all.

Griff was just finishing the wood carving when Billy Sawyer staggered to his side, the lower half of his boyish face caked in dark blood. Looking at the cabin boy, Griff had felt annoyance. Billy was weak, and the only thing that would make him strong was to fight better men than himself until he learned how to fight well. Only then would Billy Sawyer become a real sailor, a man respected enough to become a bosun's mate like his stout-hearted father.

Griff liked the boy. He had studied Billy and found him good of heart and eager to do well. But it was Griff's strong opinion that if he protected Billy or in any way shielded him from the hard life aboard ship, he would be permanently ruined, just like anything protected became weaker and weaker until it was destroyed.

Griff Hastings despised weakness wherever he saw it—in men, in birds, in animals and even in the creatures of the sea. There were some fools who believed that only men were either weak or strong. Not so. There were cowardly birds, cowardly porpoises, cowardly whales. Animals had personalities, dominant or submissive, sneaky or bold. They were more like people than most humans suspected.

Billy Sawyer was weak but he was no coward, and Griff Hastings hoped that, if the cabin boy survived a few more years, he would become strong.

"Griff, I need your help!" Billy stammered, his breath coming fast.

"No," Griff said. "Whoever did that to you, you should hurt. But I won't fight your battles."

Billy swallowed noisily. "But it's not my battle this time! It's a *woman's* battle. A rich and beautiful woman! Her name is Miss Jessica Starbuck. Griff, she owns the Circle Star fleet of merchant trading ships, and she's been shanghaied!"

The wooden duck Griff held fell from his strong hands and the first mate sat up quickly. He reached out and grabbed Billy's shoulder. "Where would you meet such a woman?"

When Billy had explained everything, Griff released his grip on the young cabin boy. "It doesn't make sense. What would a woman like that be doing in a Barbary Coast saloon?"

"Looking for a man like you!" Billy blurted, his eyes filled with such pride and admiration that Griff felt embarrassment. "That's what she was doing, Griff. She told me she needed a fighter. A man unafraid. I thought of you. She wanted to know if you were ever a pirate."

Griff actually smiled. "And you told her?"

"I said no. But I was thinkin' even as I said it that you had the heart of a pirate."

Griff admired that statement. He eased out of his berth and slipped on his shoes and then his coat. He reached under his blanket and found a gun and a dagger. He jammed both under his belt and then shrugged into a seaman's heavy jacket. "Who took her from you?"

"I don't know their names. She killed one."

Griff blinked with surprise. Rich women did not kill waterfront thugs! "Tell me how."

"She had a derringer, and she shot him right between the eyes!"

Griff could not hide his shock and admiration. "Is she young, old, pretty or . . ."

"Young and beautiful," Billy said in an almost reverent voice.

Griff had heard more than enough. His blood was already coursing with excitement as he prepared to leave. "Do you know who shanghaied her?"

"No," Billy said. "But the one that did is the one that caught me with a lucky punch and broke my damned nose! When I catch up to him, I'll—"

"Where did it happen?"

The moment Billy told him, Griff Hastings was moving. He went topside and strode across the deck to leap onto the dock.

"Wait!" Billy shouted, running after him.

Griff frowned. He debated whether or not to order the cabin boy back to the ship. He decided that Billy needed to come in order to salvage his own pride. And who could say but what the young man might not even be of some help? Not likely, but not an impossibility either.

They reached the saloon within ten minutes, and when they stepped inside, the dead man was still lying where he had fallen, though the table and chairs were now occupied.

"That's him over there!" Billy said with excitement.

"The one who shanghaied Miss Starbuck?"

"No!" Billy cried. "The one she shot between the eyes!"

"I had already figured that out for myself," Griff said

117

with disgust as he walked over to study the body.

"I don't recognize him." Griff turned his attention to three sailors that were watching him closely. "Any of you know who this swine was?"

One of the men, a bull-necked ship's cook, growled, "I might. Then again, I might not. What's it worth to find out, bub?"

Griff's fist shot out and punched into the man's throat, paralyzing him for a moment. The cook's mouth flew open, and he discovered to his horror that he could not suck air into his lungs. The man's friends reached for their guns, but Griff was faster. His own gun was in their faces and he whispered, "Your friend can't talk so good anymore. Will one of you helpful gentlemen tell me who the dead meat on the floor used to be?"

"His name was Eli Green."

"And who did he come in with?"

"Luther Tripe."

Griff cocked his weapon. "Where did Luther take the woman?"

They both shook their heads.

Griff pistol-whipped one man and grabbed the other by the ear and dragged him to his feet. He shoved the barrel of his pistol in his mouth. "Live or die. It's up to you. Where did they take the woman?"

The man's eyes grew wide with terror. He tried to talk around the barrel of the pistol, but his garbled words were incomprehensible.

Griff removed the barrel from the man's mouth. "Where is she?" he asked, his voice as gentle as a ghost floating across a country graveyard.

"I think . . . I think they took her to the frigate *Gambon*. She's preparing to sail with the tide."

Griff stepped back and motioned for Billy to head for

the door. The man whose throat he had nearly crushed was making strange whistling noises. He would live, but he would never forget to answer Griff again.

Outside the air was chill and the fog was thickening. Billy hurried along after Griff. "What now? The *Gambon?*"

"Yes. I know that ship and its captain. They're rogues and worse. They'll ransom Miss Starbuck off and then slit her throat once they have the money."

"But how do we get aboard her without being caught?"

"*You* don't," Griff said.

"But—"

Griff placed a hand on the lad's shoulder. "If the ship sails, it means I've failed, Billy. And if I have failed, then you are the only one who has any chance of saving Miss Starbuck. Go to the authorities. Tell them what happened. And if they do nothing, then go to the Starbuck offices and tell the manager what happened."

Billy's thin shoulders drooped with disappointment. "But I wanted to help you rescue her."

They approached the end of the pier. Griff looked out into the bay but he could not see the *Gambon* through the deepening layer of marine fog. He decided to row a dinghy out into the bay and take to the water only if he saw a watchman on deck. There were sharks in the water here, and a terribly strong current that would carry a swimmer to sea.

"The sharks out there don't need to dine on both of us, do they?"

Billy shivered in the fog. He studied the dark, choppy bay water. "No," he said finally. "I guess they don't."

Griff found a dinghy. He set the oars in their locks and Billy cast off for him. They waved at each other. Then

119

Griff put his powerful shoulders to the oars and was soon lost to the foggy bay.

As always when he was heading into trouble against overwhelming odds, Griff Hastings felt a strange but ever recurring mixture of fear and invincibility. One seemed to feed the other, driving his spirits up and down, and the closer he came to the exact point of danger, the more the feeling of invincibility dominated the one of fear, until he could act with calm, deadly assurance. He rowed steadily for a quarter of an hour until he saw the murky outline of the *Gambon*. She was dark and riding high in the water. Griff stopped rowing and allowed the dinghy to glide in toward the sinister looking vessel. The *Gambon* was well known for its acts of piracy and smuggling. It had once been a notorious slave ship, and Griff had sworn never to set foot, much less sail, on such vessels, for they were forever cursed by the dead Africans who had died gasping for fresh air and food down in the fetid, stinking holds.

But now there was no choice about the course his action must take. Griff craned his head back and studied the railing up above. He saw no sign of movement, or of a watchman. He dipped his oars silently until he came up to another dinghy tied at the end of a rope ladder. No doubt this was how they had taken Jessica Starbuck topside.

Griff jumped for the rope ladder and went up it as nimbly as an ape. When his head lifted above the deck of the *Gambon,* his eyes surveyed everything and missed nothing. He saw two watchmen on the deck, both smoking cigarettes, huddled against the chill of the damp, foggy night air, collars turned up. Griff consulted his pocket watch. It was 3:55 A.M., and the last night watch would be coming on in five minutes to relieve this bored pair. There was little time to waste.

He slipped under the railing and onto the deck, glad that

120

he had decided not to swim the last few yards to this ship. If he had done so, his clothes would be sopping wet and his hands would be numb and less able to do their work. Griff took a short length of pipe out from the inside of his heavy woolen sea jacket. Because of Miss Starbuck, he was going to play this safe and take no chances. He moved very swiftly now. He came at the pair, who were huddled close together in conversation. The pipe came down solidly on the base of the closer man's neck, paralyzing him instantly. Before the second watchman could even open his mouth to shout a strangled cry of warning, Griff drove the pipe up into his solar plexus. When the man jackknifed, Griff swatted him across the skull. The man hit the deck with his face. Griff stooped to drag them to the edge of the deck and toss them into the bay, but then he heard footsteps coming up from below.

It was the relief watch! Griff cursed. Usually such a watch could be expected to be at least ten or fifteen minutes late. Damn his luck that this one should be on time! There wasn't even time to get the bodies out of sight.

But the two relief watchmen were groggy and still half asleep. Heads down, they clomped up the ladder, and Griff jumped at them the moment they were both on deck. The first man never knew what hit him, but the second screamed and fell backwards. He tumbled down into the forecastle of the *Gambon* to the sleeping quarters. Griff went down after him. The bloody fool was shouting so loudly that his shipmates were all coming awake. Griff landed squarely on the man's chest and squashed the yell right out of him. But there were more sailors on board than he had expected, and when a lamp was lighted and they saw him standing over one of their mates, they came flying out of their narrow berths.

Griff drew his gun and took aim on the lantern. His

bullet plunged the deck into darkness. When the first man hit him, Griff rolled with the punch. He fired point-blank into the man's belly, and the sailor's grip fell away. Another lamp was lit and Griff shot that one out, too. Then he scrambled up the stairway. When he reached the deck, men were clawing blindly at his heels. Griff barely had time to slam the hatch down and secure it firmly.

He could feel the hatch shake, and the muffled shouts of the sailors were plainly audible. "This is what I should have done in the first place," he said aloud, though he knew that the sailors would manage to chop their way out in a very short while.

He reloaded and then headed for the captain's cabin. If this Luther Tripe and his fellow officers had heard the gunfire, Griff figured he was in real trouble. They would certainly use Miss Starbuck for a shield, and he would have a devil of a time getting her free.

The door of the captain's cabin was standing wide open and the passageway leading to that door was bathed in lamplight. Griff stopped and debated for a moment. He thought he could hear the sound of the sailors chopping madly at the hatchway. There was no time to deliberate his limited options. There was only time to act. Griff moved forward. He had the feeling that he was walking straight into a trap.

He was right. They had all heard the muffled gunshots, and now, as Luther held Jessie pinioned to his chest with a gag crammed halfway down her throat, they were like cats waiting for the mouse. Jessie's mind worked frantically. She knew there would be no second chance for her life. Ki was far away, and she would be executed before he could have any chance of rescuing her. Besides Luther, there was the repugnant captain and one other man in the room. They had been sitting at a small table, grilling her about her empire, trying to imagine how much money she was really worth and failing completely. Just before the gunshots, they had decided to ask for three hundred thousand dollars. One hundred for each.

But now the talk of money was over. Guns were drawn. Jessie could taste the rancid breath of Luther Tripe in her nostrils and it made her want to vomit. This entire ship had a stench that was almost unimaginable and which gave her the chills.

I have to do something right now! she cried to herself. *Right now!*

Jessie raised her foot to knee level and jumped up, scraping the rigid edge of her sole down Luther's shin. Unable to drive her knee into his groin because he held her so close, unable to rake his eyes because her hands were bound behind her back, it was her only hope. Ki had once shown her that technique and had himself used it though his ankles had also been bound, making the feat much more difficult. Ki had promised Jessie that, if the thing were done correctly, it would cause excruciating pain.

Ki had not been exaggerating. Luther howled, and when the pressure of his powerful arms slackened, Jessie tilted her head back and slammed it into his nose as hard as she could. Everything that happened next was too fast to understand. She heard a savage, blood-chilling roar, and then bullets were flying in all directions. The cabin was plunged into darkness. Jessie struggled to break free from Luther, but the man's fingers caught in her hair and his sole intention seemed to be to shield himself from death.

"No, Griff, no!" he bellowed.

In the very next instant Jessie felt warm blood, and she heard Luther gurgle and choke. Jessie pulled away and staggered, almost falling, but someone caught her and held her up. "Let's get out of here, Miss Starbuck, while the dogs of hell are still in their cage."

With a gag rammed down her throat, Luther's blood smeared across her cheek, and her nostrils filled with gunsmoke, Jessie had never wanted anything more in her entire life. She felt herself being propelled into the passageway and then up dark stairs into the chill, foggy night air.

Only now did Griff stop for a moment to look at her. He yanked the gag out of her mouth, and while she tried to inhale fresh air as quickly as possible, he untied the rope that bound her wrists. That finished, he jumped over to the hatch. Jessie saw that the wood had already been partly chopped away by the trapped sailors below, and the hole was being expanded with every blow of an axe. Still, it was not quite large enough for anyone to be able to reach an arm through and unbolt the latch. Griff shoved the muzzle of his gun into the hole and emptied his pistol directly into the faces of those standing on the ladder.

Jessie heard terrible screams. She almost tripped over two bodies, and then she saw the tall, powerful first mate come bounding to her side.

"If we had more time, we could really make things difficult for them," he said a little wistfully.

"You've done enough," Jessie gasped. "Let's get off this stinking deathtrap!"

"Right," he said.

And before she quite knew what to expect, he scooped her up and tossed her over his shoulder, just the way Luther Tripe had done hours before. Jessie shouted at him in anger and started to beat at his back, but they dropped over the side of the *Gambon* and a scream built up in her throat until she realized that he was grabbing a rope ladder and that there was actually a small boat directly below.

124

He dropped her in the stern and grabbed the oars. "Enjoy the ride," he said with a smile. "The excitement is all over for tonight."

Jessie slumped down in the small rowboat. There were two inches of water in it that sloshed back and forth as Griff Hastings put his back to the task of delivering them safely to the waterfront. She was cold, pummeled, smeared, and covered with the foul odor of the death-ship that Griff Hastings had singlehandedly almost destroyed.

And even though she was annoyed by his high-handed ways, she knew that she had found exactly the man she needed at Lake Tahoe. All that was required now was to get this amazing fellow to leave the sea for a while.

Chapter 12

Billy Sawyer was waiting for them on the wharf. When he saw Jessie and the blood on her face, he thought for sure she had been cut or shot and was close to dying.

"I'm all right," Jessie said, "thanks to the both of you."

Billy helped her out of the dinghy. "I didn't do much of anything," he said. "It was all Griff, as usual."

"That's not true," the first mate said, stepping lightly up onto the pier and taking Jessie's arm. "It was team effort. Miss Starbuck, if you hadn't acted like you did, I'd never have gotten through the captain's doorway."

"I'm just grateful this is all over," Jessie told the two men, who each took one of her arms and escorted her up the dark and fog-shrouded avenue towards the more re-spectable part of town, where she was staying. "But I would have to say, Griff, that you are as terrible a man in a fight as Ki."

"Who?"

"Ki," Jessie repeated. "He's my friend and companion. He's a samurai."

Billy did not know the meaning of the word, but Griff understood completely. "Well," he said, "I don't measure up too well against a true samurai. I once fought beside a couple of them in the Japans. When the fight was over, I was glad that I had picked their side of the battle and not

127

opposed them. They're as fine a fighting bunch as has ever been seen on this planet."

"Yes," Jessie said, "but I think you're their equal. Did Billy tell you that I would need to hire a captain who knows logging?"

Griff shook his head. "Our conversation was pretty brief."

"Well, I do, and I think you're the man for the job."

"Why?"

"Because he told me that your father owns a logging business in Seattle, and that you know nearly as much about timber as you do about the sea."

Griff shook his head and frowned at Billy. "Sometimes Billy exaggerates."

"Uh-uh," Jessie said. "He also told me that you were a fighter, a man without fear, and the best friend anyone could have. Also the worst kind of enemy."

"Billy also talks too damn much," Griff said, an edge creeping into his voice.

"Not to my way of thinking," Jessie said. "You proved his words right down the line tonight. I want you for the job."

The tall man shrugged his wide rack of shoulders. "I'm just a first mate, but I do know a few things about logging. Where is this job of yours? Pacific Northwest?"

"Lake Tahoe."

He stopped dead in his tracks. "At the top of the Sierras! Why, no, ma'am! I'm a seaman and I've never even been in the mountains. I'd probably get dizzy or weak up there, where the air is so thin and cold."

"No you wouldn't," Jessie argued. "I have a stern-wheel steamer that's just been shot halfway off a beach by cannon. There's going to be a timber war on the water and I need a fighting captain to lead a fighting crew, Mr. Hastings. And you are a fighter."

But Griff was not convinced. The idea of going up into the cold mountains, with their high, thin air, leaving the salt sea spray and the rolling tides behind, was not to his liking.

"I just don't think I'm the man for it," he confessed. "But I can give you some bold seafarers who would be up to the task. And a crew shouldn't be hard to come up with."

"I want to be one of them," Billy said eagerly. "I'll come up to the mountains and fight for you, Miss Starbuck."

Jessie didn't have the heart to tell Billy no. "If you're sure."

"I'm dead sure."

They had reached Jessie's hotel room. She paused beside the front entrance, not willing to let Griff off so easily. "Will you come to join me for supper tomorrow evening, Griff?"

"I told you," he said stubbornly, "I just don't think I'm your man for the mountains."

"Then bring me a list of men who might feel differently," she said. "Please?"

Griff nodded. "What time?"

"In twelve hours from now."

He nodded and started to go, but she reached out and touched his arm. "And if you and Billy could help me find a crew of fighting sailors and some cannon to buy for transport up to Lake Tahoe, that would be helpful."

He frowned. "You said your stern-wheeler was blown apart. What are you going to do with a cannon?"

"The samurai and another friend are rebuilding the vessel right now. They are risking their lives to put it back together so that a man like you can captain it. But I must confess something, Griff. It's only my one vessel against three just as large, with eight-pound cannon mounted port and starboard."

The first mate took a deep breath. "There's no way you can win a naval battle. Sure, you'll need the cannon; but to win, whoever is in command will have to whittle the odds down some. He'd best not try and wait until all three corner him."

"Then you think . . ."

"I think you had better hire a captain who will take the fight to your enemies and catch those ships one by one and sink 'em without showing any mercy."

Jessie nodded. "Thank you for your naval strategy, Mr. Hastings. Billy, if you want to help, you are on my payroll starting tomorrow. You know where my maritime office is."

"Yes, ma'am."

"Tell them what I've said. And I'll put you in charge of finding us cannon. We need . . . how many, Mr. Hastings?"

"How long is your vessel?"

"Seventy feet."

"Solid decks?"

Jessie nodded. "My samurai will have replaced the decks with ponderosa pine by the time we return."

Griff nodded. "Then four eight-pounders ought to be enough, and if—"

"Thank you, Mr. Hastings," Jessica said, purposefully cutting him off in mid-sentence. It was her belief that this first mate was a little too sure of himself, and she wanted him to leave her feeling that he could have—even should have—offered her more. That way he would be certain to anticipate returning this evening.

Jessie hurried into the plush hotel. When the night clerk

130

saw the blood-smear on her lovely face, his sleepy eyes popped wide open. "Miss Starbuck," he cried, "shall I summon a physician?"

"No. Just make sure your boilers are able to deliver hot water for a bath. Lots and lots of hot water!"

Jessie slept for a solid eight hours after her long and luxurious bath. When she awoke it was late afternoon and the street below was filled with traffic. She was hungry but not famished, and she dressed very carefully in a white chiffon outfit with a rather daring neckline. She wore pearl earrings but decided not to wear a diamond ring. She wanted to impress Mr. Hastings, not overwhelm him with her station or wealth.

Griff arrived on time. To her delight, he was well dressed in a civilian suit that had been hand-woven and beautifully tailored in the Orient. His starched shirt was silk, but the collar seemed to bother him a little. They went at once to dinner in the hotel.

The waiter brought them champagne and took their order. Griff could not seem to take his eyes off of her, and Jessie felt warmed by his approving gaze. "My dear Miss Starbuck," he whispered as they toasted each other's health and long life, "you are stunning!"

"Thank you. You are a very attractive man yourself, Mr. Hastings. And a very brave and resourceful one. Those are rare combinations."

"I lead a charmed life," he told her. "I'm a man of some ability, but by all rights, I should have been killed dozens of times before now."

"You can call it a 'charmed life' if you choose to do so," Jessie told him. "Others would say they were lucky. In both cases, I would disagree. Men like you and Ki are extraordinary not because of good fortune but because you

131

are natural fighters, men who have magnificent reflexes, great speed and strength, and are absolutely fearless in battle."

It was Griff's turn to blush now. "Are you sure you haven't left anything out, Miss Starbuck?"

"Of course I have," she told him. "Please, let's use first names. And I'd like to see that list you brought of possible sea captains."

Griff made no move to produce a list. "Tell me," he said, acting as if he had not heard the request. "Why is it so important for you to have a stern-wheeler on Lake Tahoe?"

Jessie explained to him all about the Comstock Lode miners who were daily being buried alive for lack of good timbering, and how the Lode itself was in danger of being shut down. She also told Griff about her violent encounters with the Yoders.

"You mean one of them actually tried to open your blouse and . . ."

"He paid dearly for it. I'm afraid that, between Ki and me, he had difficulty walking for a while."

The first mate laughed loud enough so that the other diners in the room turned their heads. Griff realized he was attracting their attention and he waved at them. "The trouble with a room full of people that have a lot of money is they always turn out to be a bunch of stuffed shirts. Why, go to a sailor's tavern or cafe with this many people in it and you'll hear nothing but laughter."

"I've been to a sailor's tavern," Jessie said. "Last evening. Remember?"

"That's right," he said. "I'd forgotten. But that wasn't a tavern, ma'am. That was more like an eel's den. You couldn't have picked a worse place to go. I gave Billy hell for even allowing you inside."

"He really didn't have any choice." Jessie sipped her

chilled champagne and looked into his eyes. "Griff, I won't mince words with you, or try to charm you or anything at all. I will simply say that I need your help and I'm willing to pay any price to receive it."

"I have list of five captains who—"

"I don't want to see it!" Jessie cried with exasperation. "Just name your price."

Griff downed his champagne and poured himself more. "My price might not be what you'd expect."

"Name it," Jessie said, looking boldly into his eyes.

"You know what it is."

Jessie felt a shiver pass through her body as his eyes dropped to her cleavage.

"And this dinner along with another bottle of this champagne to go," he added with a wide smile as if he'd just struck a terrible bargain.

Jessie's lips parted. "You have a deal, Griff."

He blinked and he seemed surprised. "Are you sure?"

"Very," she told him with complete honesty.

"Then to Lake Tahoe and your damned old timber war," he said, raising his glass in a toast. "And to our swift and satisfying victory."

Jessie's crystal glass tinkled against his own. "Yes," she said, suddenly feeling very, very hungry.

They had spoken little over their fine dinner of shrimp, frog's legs, and baby carrots in a wonderful French sauce followed by cherries jubilee. They had finished their meal without hurry but also without unnecessary delay. Jessie had paid the bill and ordered a second bottle of champagne on ice delivered to her suite.

And now, as Griff opened that bottle and filled their glasses, Jessie slowly began to undress. He watched her with keen intent, his eyes full of her, his chest rising and falling as if he had already began to exert himself. When her dress fell to her ankles, Griff tossed down his glass of champagne and dried his lips with the cuff of his sleeve.

"I've had a lot of women," he said, "some good, some bad, but none so beautiful as you."

Jessie removed her chemise and then slipped out of her underclothes to stand before him like a prize.

"Please turn completely around," he asked, setting her glass on the bedside table.

Jessie turned around very slowly as his eyes feasted on her every curve. He noted the smooth line of her legs, the little tuck of her buttocks, and the beautiful line of narrow hips that melded up into her full breasts. When she had made a full circle, she regarded him with a tantalizing smile.

"Seen enough, Captain Hastings?"

In answer, Griff reached out, took her head by the back of her neck, and pulled her mouth to his own. His kiss inflamed Jessie and she melted against him with a driving hunger firing her loins.

Griff stepped back and undressed quickly as Jessie turned the bedspread. She wanted this man badly, not only because she was convinced he was the only person alive who could successfully captain her fledgling logging operation, but because he had risked his own life to save hers.

"Come here," she ordered him when he was fully undressed and standing like a great aroused god.

Griff came to her side and she pushed him gently back on the bed. Jessie bent and kissed him for a long moment, then knelt over him, her long fingers roaming his rippling muscles. His erection was a pulsing tower, but she ignored it for a few moments as she straddled his chest and leaned forward. He reached up and pulled her downward, his lips finding her already hardened nipples. He teased them with

134

his mouth and his tongue as he went from one to the other. Jessie smiled with delight.

"Oh," she whispered, rubbing herself hard against his chest and feeling waves of pleasure radiate upward from her honeypot, "that feels good!"

Griff's fingers slipped downward and found the point of her most intense pleasure. His finger slipped inside of her. She was already slick and juicy. Unbidden, her hips began to rotate around and around, and his tongue worked faster on her nipples, inciting her to greater passion. For one of the first times in her life, Jessie realized that she would have to slow down or she was going to climax long before her man.

She raised her hips and pulled his hand away. He mistook her intention, and before she could indicate that she needed to slow her spiraling passion, he clamped his hands on her hips and drove his massive erection straight upward.

Impaled, Jessie felt her mouth fly open and her eyelids flutter. She gasped and collapsed against his chest. He rolled over on top of her and then pushed himself up until his elbows were locked at her sides. His powerful hips were moving in long, deep thrusts that were driving her wild.

Looking down at her with eyes glazed with desire, Griff whispered, "Is this how you like it, Jessie?"

Jessie felt as if her womanhood was on fire with the most exquisitely beautiful pain imaginable. Her head rolled back and forth on her pillow and her fingernails dug into his muscled buttocks, pulling him deeper and deeper into her. "Don't do anything different," she begged, "and please don't stop!"

Griff threw back his head and laughed. His head bent and he sucked on her aching breasts while his huge organ stirred her toward the brink of sweet madness. Jessie's

135

heels began to move up and down on the satin sheets. She could not seem to get enough of this seaman!

Suddenly, she felt a scream building in her throat. Her head began to swim and she nearly fainted as a monstrous wave of pleasure washed over her like a rolling tidal wave. Her body went out of control, and as the cry rose up from her throat, Griff capped it with his mouth and his body clamped down on hers like a vise. It also began to spasm with powerful thrusts, and Jessie felt their hot juices flooding together as they locked in a frenzied embrace that seemed to have no beginning and no end.

Jessie would never tell this man, but she would not have missed this lovemaking for anything. And whether or not Captain Griff Hastings was yet aware of it, he was going to be earning his keep both day and night at Lake Tahoe.

Chapter 13

They were finished. The samurai placed his hammer and saw on the newly constructed deck of the *Tahoe* and turned to stare out at the lake. His dark, almond-shaped eyes squinted at the bright water, and his gaze roamed the miles of lake surface, looking for one of the Yoder vessels to come steaming in off the horizon. If that happened, he would be helpless. The *Tahoe* was completely vulnerable, and their work would be wasted. They would have slaved all this time for nothing. He would have failed Jessie, who had given him the responsibility of having this vessel ready. It was ready. Ki knew his sole task now was to keep it that way.

Beside him, Ken Bell finished up the last touches of paint and said, "You expect trouble at any minute, don't you."

"Yes," Ki said. "We've seen a Yoder ship steam past this cove every day for the last week, and they've been watching the repair work closely. The last two days, nothing. To my mind, that seems to say that they think we might relax our guard."

"If they're going to come back and blow this vessel apart with their cannon again, what are they waiting for? Why don't they just do it and be done with the suspense?"

Ki shrugged. "The best way to break a man's fighting

spirit is to crush him at the very last minute. Let him think he has a chance, even a thread of hope, then deliver the final, crushing blow. I'd say that's what Yoder is doing."

Ken looked defeated. "I don't even know myself why we're bothering to do this. You know this vessel doesn't stand a chance out on the lake. Hell, three to one against her. Even with cannon, all they have to do is corner us and blast us right out of the water."

Ki agreed. He had been thinking about this for a good long while, and he had reached the conclusion that their only defense was an offense. "Can I buy dynamite from anyone up here besides Scotty?"

Ken looked at him strangely. "Why do you ask?"

"Because," the samurai said, "I'm going to even the odds."

"You mean, you want to blow up the . . ." He shook his head as if he could not even imagine Ki's daring plan. "You mean you want to blow up the Yoder side-wheelers?"

"As many as I can." Ki shrugged his shoulders. "Why not? Dynamite ought to do as well as cannon."

"You haven't got the chance of a snowball in hell of getting close to those vessels in the first place. And in the second, how would you escape?"

"Same way I plan on getting to them. By canoe. So I'll need to buy one of those along with the dynamite. But I'll have to charge it to Circle Star. Jessie has control of the money. I rarely need any."

Ken exhaled deeply. "Attempt this crazy plan and you'll never need anything again."

Ki turned his attention back to the lake. "I think they will attack very soon. Maybe this evening or tomorrow. I can't afford to wait any longer. This ship is repaired and ready to operate. It won't be so hard to get her down into

138

the water again. See if you can hire the men and animals to do it tomorrow."

"Tomorrow." Ken threw up his hands. "Just like that you say, tomorrow. I'll tell you something, samurai. You've proven yourself a pretty good man in a fight and also with woodworking tools. But nothing short of the United States Navy could stop Yoder and his ships from destroying us tomorrow if they even suspect that you might use dynamite on them."

It was obvious to Ki that Ken Bell was a pessimist who always seemed to look at the worst side of things. He assumed everything was going to go wrong, and perhaps that assumption was based on his own personal failures. But Ki looked at things exactly the opposite. He presumed success and expected victory.

"I have much to do," Ki said. "How far will I need to paddle in order to reach the place where our enemy docks his ships?"

Ken shook his head, but under Ki's steady gaze, he raised his finger and pointed north. "Clinton Yoder owns an old rock fortress that is sitting on a peninsula that juts right out over the water. You'll have to row around that fortress and then you'll find a big cove of water. There's a sawmill and pier coming right out into the water about two hundred feet. That's where the side-wheelers will be docked. And they'll be well guarded. Everything is well guarded."

"Maybe it's only guarded from a *land* attack," Ki said. "Maybe they won't be expecting trouble from across the water."

"No," Ed agreed, "they probably won't. I mean, after all, you'll only have to paddle your damned canoe about twenty miles to get there. And unless you have a back of steel and hands that are tougher than hide, you'll be a goner by then."

139

Ki had heard enough. "When I get back, we will need to move this vessel to a safer harbor. I doubt if I can destroy all three vessels. Maybe I'll only get one or two."

"Hey!"

Ki had started to leave but now he turned. Ken Bell might be a complainer, but the one-legged man was no coward, and he had driven himself just as hard as Ki to completely rebuild the stern and paddle-wheel of this ship. Ki could not have done it alone.

"Hey," Ken said quietly, "you want me to come along? I'm a pretty good shot with a rifle. Maybe I could make a difference."

"Of course you could. But you'll make an even bigger one here. Get this damned thing in the water and get it out of Hunter's Cove tomorrow morning, Ken. The way I see it, they are going to come after it one way or the other. Until Jessie returns, the only hope we have is in hitting them first and hitting them hard. That, and playing cat-and-mouse until Jessie returns with cannon and a sea cap-tain."

"I'll do it," Ken promised. "I'll keep up my part of it. But I don't see how anyone could paddle twenty miles at a stretch and then . . ."

Ki turned and left the man. It was only a little after noon, but time was already running short. And if he had judged it wrong and the Yoders were already steaming down the lake to annihilate the *Tahoe,* then there was little he could do to stop them. He would have failed Jessie and failed himself.

The samurai was in a hurry.

"You want to buy that?" Scotty asked as if he had not heard.

"Keep your voice down," the samurai said. "I don't

140

want someone to overhear us and then warn the Yoders. I just want dynamite and fuses and a good fast canoe."

"But you have no cash," Scotty said, leaning across his bar and dropping his voice.

"That's right. But you know Miss Starbuck will make good on payment."

"What she'll do is take a gun or a knife to me when she finds out that I sent you off alone. You don't have a chance!"

"And neither," Ki said very deliberately, "does the *Tahoe,* if I don't disable all three of Yoders' side-wheelers before they come steaming up to shell us again."

Scotty scratched his whiskers. "Hmm," he mused. "I reckon I can't argue with that any."

"Then you'll do it?"

"I will," the old saloon owner said, "but not 'cause I want to. It's just that I have no choice."

"And neither do I," the samurai told him. "I've got a long way to go and not much time to get there, so I'd like to get started."

Scotty called for a man to take his place behind the bar. He walked into his general store and then into a back storage room. "Old Clinton will know it was me who gave you the dynamite and the canoe. So you better hit 'em hard and don't mess it up any. With them cannons of his, he could loft cannon balls right through my roof. Destroy this place in a helluva hurry."

"I'll do my best," Ki said, as he knelt beside the man and helped him open a case of dynamite and remove the sawdust packing.

"How many do you need?"

"Nine," the samurai said. "Three for each vessel."

"Better take an extra," Scotty advised, counting out ten. "You might need it to get yourself out of a scrape. Just

141

remember, if you do get in trouble, throw this stuff into the lake. I reckon old Clinton has some of his own, but I sure don't want to add to his store. I'll give you ten feet of fuse. That ought to be enough to do whatever you need to do."

"It will," Ki said, taking the dynamite and fuse and cramming it into a waterproof oilskin sack.

"Make sure you have matches and flint, just in case you get them wet."

"I already do," Ki said, dropping the matches in with the dynamite.

"Let's go out the back way and right down to the lake," Scotty said. "Wouldn't do to have everyone in my place see you walking out of here with all that explosive."

Ki agreed completely. He had no doubt in his mind that the Yoders had replaced their earlier informants with fresh ones. They walked quickly down to the water and stepped onto the dock. "There it is," he said, "the only canoe I own. Hasn't been used this year. When I was younger, I used to take ladies out for a ride on the lake and then pretend like I didn't know how to handle the damned tipsy thing. I'd tip it over right close to shore somewhere beside a beach. Damned if the lady wouldn't have to take off her clothes and dry them in the sun. One thing would lead to another, and we'd have us a high old time." Scotty sighed, remembering. "Yes sir, I sure did use that canoe to advantage. But it got so that everybody knew that when I took a woman out in it I was gonna tip it over. Hell, they'd line up at the dock and hoot and cheer so bad that no respectable woman would get close to the damned thing. And even them that *wasn't* so respectable would shy away from here. That water is mighty cold. No woman liked the dunking. Just what came later."

Scotty cackled to himself while Ki studied the canoe. It was made of pine and it wasn't pretty, but it looked sound so he placed the sack of dynamite down on the pier before he climbed into the craft. It rocked gently but seemed watertight. There was a paddle resting in the bow and he picked it up and inspected it carefully. "This will be fine."

"I don't expect to ever see it again," Scotty said, handing him the sack. "What about weapons?"

"Mine are hidden in the rocks just downshore," Ki answered. "I'll pick them up on my way."

"Well, good luck. I personally think you're one dead warrior. And I'm going to be a nervous sonofabitch until I see if you pull this off or not."

"I'll succeed," Ki said. "But Ken Bell is going to be trying to get the *Tahoe* off the beach and he could use some help."

Scotty nodded. "I'll gather up men and animals. It shouldn't be so tough dragging her down to the water and getting her afloat. In fact, if we can do that, I'll even get my old buffalo rifle and help keep guard."

"Do that," Ki said as he pushed off and paddled away. The canoe moved well in the water. It handled beautifully and rode light and high. Ki knew how to paddle one, for he had done it before. He considered canoes greatly superior to rowboats.

He paddled over to the rocks and jumped to the shore, where he collected his bow and quiver of arrows. Then he headed north along the shore, paddling smoothly and with as little wasted effort as possible. The sun was warm on his face. He could see big fish scurry into the dark holes and crevices for cover as his canoe passed swiftly over their heads. It was a fine day. A good day to go to war.

Ki threw his head back, closed his eyes, and smiled up at the sun. He said a silent prayer that he would reach the three Yoder vessels sometime soon after dark and that he would find them unguarded.

But even if they were guarded, the samurai knew that he would still prevail against his enemies. He was a *ninja*. He knew the art of the invisible assassin and he could not, would not, fail.

Hour after hour the samurai paddled. The afternoon sun penetrated the thin atmosphere and burned the back of his neck and his forearms. Sweat trickled down his spine and his muscles began to cramp as the sun dove toward the western rim of the basin. But Ki pushed out all thoughts of his own discomfort, and his mind focused primarily on the task that lay just ahead. He thought of Jessie and tried not to worry about her. It was unusual that he should leave her unprotected and exposed to danger, but it had been her wish that he remain here and finish repairing their stern-wheeler. Now that was accomplished, and he was about to take the equally important second step of protecting that vessel.

The sunset was as spectacular as any the samurai had ever seen, and he marveled at the colors and he drew calmness from them. Far ahead, he could see the long peninsula and the first lights that blinked from the windows of the rock fortress of the Yoders. Had it not been that he knew his primary responsibility was to destroy or at least incapacitate the three vessels, Ki would have been tempted to pay that family a visit and perhaps persuade them to change their way of doing business. The devastating cannon barrage and the resulting destruction of the *Tahoe* had been unforgivable. It had been a miracle that no one was killed. If there had been, Ki knew that he and Jessie would have exacted swift retribution.

Darkness fell swiftly. One by one the stars appeared, and then the moon glowed softly in the heavens. The samurai paddled wide of the peninsula and then angled toward the cove, his eyes never leaving the three big silhouettes of the stern-wheelers. He saw lights on them, and once or twice men walking up and down the long pier to which they were moored.

When Ki was still a mile out from the end of the pier, he stooped very low in the bow of his canoe and paddled carefully. Not a sound could be heard from his dipping and lifting oars as the canoe slipped across the dark water toward the pier. Ki aimed right at the end of the pier, and the canoe swept quietly under it and glided until it gently bumped into a piling. The water lapped against the pilings, but otherwise there was not a sound.

Ki sat in his canoe and considered his next move. The three stern-wheelers were docked close together. Ki had imagined he would tie dynamite to their paddle-wheels, but now he saw that was impractical. All the paddle-wheels were on the same side, and therefore it would be impossible to go from one to the other quickly; to reach them he would have to go completely around each vessel.

Ki decided that he had no choice but to board the middle vessel, then light sticks of dynamite and hurl them at the other two stern-wheelers from atop the second deck. If he could lob the sticks of dynamite into the paddle-works, then he could wreck their paddles and render them just as useless as the *Tahoe* had been for the last couple of weeks.

There was no other way. He didn't have enough fuse to try and set all three charges of dynamite so that they went off before Yoder's men could react.

Ki unwound a long piece of twine from around his wrist. Working in almost total darkness under the pier, he carefully tied together five explosive sets of two sticks each. Satisfied that he was ready, he left one bundle of dynamite in the bottom of the canoe, shoved the other four pairs back into the sack, and grabbed his bow and quiver.

Pushing the canoe back under the pier, he used a rope to tie it so that it would not drift away.

Ki moved up on the pier and lay flat on its rough surface. He looked down the pier and saw that it was empty. But all three vessels were occupied by Yoder men. Now that he was higher, he could see that there were men on every deck, smoking and talking. He had half expected that the crews might actually live on their ships, and now this suspicion confirmed itself. Down at the end of the pier, Ki heard two men approaching. Their shapes were dark but he could hear their steps thumping louder and louder. Ki knew he had to move quickly. He lifted to his feet and jumped lightly onto the middle stern-wheeler.

The samurai reached behind his back and selected an arrow. It was "Death Song," an arrow with a small ceramic head that had a hole in it. When "Death Song" flew, the wind moved through the head and emitted a terrible shriek that was almost certain to unnerve an opponent. To most men who had heard this sound, it was the combination of a giant mosquito buzzing next to your ear and the sound of a violin string being tortured by a beginning student.

"Hey!" a sailor yelled. "Who the hell are you!"

Ki had not seen the man who had been sitting quietly alone hidden by a pile of timber.

Damn! the samurai thought. He tried to bluff his way through to gain additional time. There were a lot of men on the Yoder payroll, and Bill was a very popular name. "It's Bill," he replied.

The Yoder man stood up and stared at Ki. He started to move closer, and when he saw that Ki was wearing sandals and a ninja outfit, and was carrying a very unusually shaped bow, he knew something was amiss. "Now wait just a—"

Ki had no choice. He saw the man stab for his six-gun.

146

There was no way the samurai could reach him in time to deliver a sweep-kick. Ki drew back "Death Song" and sent the deadly arrow whistling straight for the man's heart.

The arrow's sound pierced the night. Then the arrow itself buried its head into the man's chest. He slammed noisily up against the engine room.

Ki reached for another arrow, realizing that the element of surprise was gone now. Men were coming. Ki sent his next arrow, "Chewer," straight for the first one to come at him. The arrow caught the unfortunate man in the stomach and he screamed in agony. A gunshot sounded and Ki took off running for the ladder that led to the second deck. When he reached it, he removed the sack of dynamite from his shoulder and fumbled for the matches. He found them, but then he heard the sound of running footsteps coming up the ladder.

The samurai raced back to the stairs. His foot streaked upward and he caught the first man under the chin, lifting him over backward. The man dropped onto those below him and cleared the ladder all the way back down to the first deck.

But the other two crews were firing up at Ki. The only thing that saved his life was that the light was poor. Again Ki grabbed the dynamite. He ducked behind the wheelhouse and located the matches. Striking one, he touched it to the fuse as bullets ricocheted off the wheelhouse. Ki could hear the men below assaulting the ladders again. The samurai waited until the fuse had burned low, and then he dashed out and hurled the double sticks of dynamite at the vessel to his right. Hurled it directly into the paddle-wheel. Ki hit the deck as men screamed. An instant later there was an immense explosion. The paddle-wheel disintegrated and sent splintered timber high into the air to rain down on all three ships.

But men were fighting their way up to Ki's deck. Ki ran to meet them, and a *shuriken* blade flashed to lodge itself in one man's throat. He grabbed a second man and hurled him back at those behind him. The man fired his gun, and Ki felt a bullet pass through his outfit even as his foot came up, driving a flat-foot kick to the man's belly that sent him backpedaling. Ki charged the men, and his fists and hands chopped at them from many angles. Men cried out, grabbing broken faces or falling to the deck with their knees dislocated.

Again, Ki drove the men back down the ladder and then raced to the dynamite. He lit another bundle and hurried to the opposite side of the vessel. This time, he knew, he would have to make a perfect lob, over the water and clearing the beam of the vessel, in order to reach its off-side paddle-wheel. Otherwise, he would have to disable it in some other way.

Ki felt a bullet crease his arm. He charged across the deck, knowing that he was a perfect target with the burning fuse in his fist. There was no help for that. He stopped, took aim, and threw the dynamite in a hard line at the wheelhouse. The double sticks punctured the window and glass shattered. An instant later, the wheelhouse was blown to pieces.

Ki dropped and stared at the burning place where there had once been a wheelhouse. *Good work!* he thought. *They will not operate that one for at least a few weeks.*

A gun flashed behind Ki. The samurai heard a bullet whine off metal, and he threw himself sideways. Then he put another one of his precious *shuriken* blades to good use. The man's gun flashed again. But this time, it was at the stars. The fellow hit the deck and did not move.

Ki lit another and another stick of dynamite and began tossing them at both the vessel on his left and the one on

148

his right. He could hear the Yoder men shouting and diving into the lake. Fires started on both steamships, and the flames climbed higher and higher into the night sky.

Ki was down to his last two sticks of dynamite, and he knew it was time to get out of this cove. He glanced around and almost decided to hurl the dynamite down into the paddle, but he changed his mind at the last minute for something better.

Kneeling behind a piece of ironwork, Ki lit the fuse of the last two sticks and then looked up at the tall exhaust stack just a short way forward. There was no fire in the box, no heat in the boilers; but the samurai figured he'd make some of his own heat. With a grin of satisfaction creasing his lips, he raced forward to the stack. With an upward-sweeping motion of his arm, he tossed the dynamite skyward. But it bounced off the lip of the stack and fell back. With his heart in his mouth, Ki caught the dynamite and tossed it skyward once more. This time it vanished down the smokestack.

Ki grabbed his bow and arrow in his hands and took a running jump off the second deck of the ship. He was in midair when the boiler of the ship he had just launched himself from exploded with a tremendous roar.

Ki hit the water and went under. He tucked his bow and quiver under one arm and swam until he reached a piling. Then he surfaced and groped around in the dark until he found his canoe. He climbed into it and tied his last bundle of dynamite just under the pier. Working strictly by feel, he cut a long fuse. With the sound of footsteps racing directly over his head, Ki used his flint to spark fire and get the fuse going.

Most of the Yoder men were trying to extinguish the fires, but the others were looking for him out on the water. The three side-wheelers were burning so intensely that the night seemed as bright as day; Ki knew he could not escape by water across the cove. Three dozen rifles would cut him to pieces. So he did the only thing he could, which was to paddle toward shore directly between the long rows of pilings. When the canoe touched the beach, Ki removed his *tanto* knife and ripped a hole in the canoe. He sank it right under the pier and found a few heavy rocks to weight it to the bottom. With luck, the canoe would not be discovered for a long, long time.

It sounded like an army running overhead. Ki looked south, and then slung his bow and quiver over his shoulders and sank into the water and began to swim with only his head above the surface. He would skirt the peninsula and then swim a few miles in open water before he returned to shore. He just was not up to a twenty-mile swim, not after paddling all the way here.

When Ki reached the tip of the peninsula, he turned back to see the three Yoder vessels burning in the water. Suddenly the entire end of the pier buckled with a tremendous roar, and then it was gone, along with the men who had been standing over the blast.

Ki swam on. It was a long way back to Scotty and the *Tahoe*. He would have to hurry to make it by daybreak.

Chapter 14

Ki swam steadily until long after midnight, when his arms began to feel leaden and the water had chilled him right to the marrow of his bones. Then he angled into shore. When he tried to stand he was dismayed to discover that his legs had to struggle to support his weight. His teeth were chattering and his hands were so numb that he could barely remove his bow and quiver from over his head. The samurai knew that he had to warm himself before he continued on. A few hours beside a fire would revive his body and bring life back into his frozen limbs.

The samurai dragged himself up onto a beach and into the dark forest. He gathered up an armful of dry pine needles and placed them on the beach, hollowing out a bowl in the sand so that a fire could not be easily observed by the Yoders, who might even come searching for him in the night. Ki located his flint. His hands and fingers were so numb that it took him quite some time before he could get the spark he needed to set the needles afire. But when they caught, the blaze jumped up quickly, and Ki hurried back into the forest to get some dry wood. In a very few minutes, the samurai had a nice fire going. He extended his hands toward it, feeling warmth slowly begin to penetrate his flesh.

To the north, he could see only a single red glow on the water. This told the samurai that the Yoders had extinguished two of their ship's fires. But one, probably the vessel into the boiler of which he had dropped a charge of dynamite, was going to be a complete loss and burn away to the waterline.

Ki was pleased with his evening's work. He had destroyed one of the Yoder side-wheelers and had seriously damaged the remaining pair. He'd managed to hide the canoe so that it would not implicate Scotty as being a part of the sabotage. Then he had gotten away cleanly.

A warning sounded in Ki's brain. He hurriedly began to throw sand on the fire to extinguish the flames. Somewhere close by in the forest, he heard a branch snap. He knew it had not been stepped upon by a wild animal. Ki grabbed his bow and quiver. He nocked an arrow and retreated on his hands and knees back toward the lakeshore. He could not imagine how any man could have seen his fire, except perhaps an Indian or . . . a mountain man!

There were two mountain men. They came flying out of the dark trees from opposite sides of the beach. In the moon and starlight, Ki saw only their silhouettes gliding across the pale sand. One had an Indian hatchet, and the other brandished both a pistol and a knife. They were tall, rangy men in buckskin breeches and tunics. Silent, deadly men, filled with a single purpose—to track down quarry and kill it swiftly and efficiently.

Ki jumped up to one knee and put an arrow into the one with the pistol. The big fellow lost his stride in the sand and staggered. But he kept coming, and Ki knew that his arrow had not penetrated a vital organ. The second man fired his gun and Ki felt a hot pain in his side. He doubled up, and that was when he realized that the hatchet had created a long gash just under his ribs. The man jumped at Ki, and there was no time for the samurai to nock another arrow. They came together and the mountain man slammed an elbow into Ki's

152

face, rocking him back. The mountain man reached for his own knife even as Ki drove a *tegatana* blow that connected with the rock-hard edge of his tensed hand and sent the knife spinning. The man grabbed Ki by the throat and tried to break his neck. He was so powerful that it took Ki a moment to get his own hands up. But when he did, he found an *atemi* point and dug his thumb into the base of the mountain man's neck, paralyzing him instantly.

But the first mountain man was still alive and coming, despite the arrow in his chest. He roared and fell on Ki. The samurai heard the shaft of the arrow snap as he tried to grab the man's wrist and keep him from emptying his pistol downward into the samurai's face.

For a moment they locked in mortal combat. The mountain man was the stronger, but his wound was mortal and his strength was bleeding away very quickly.

"Goddamn you!" he gritted. "I'll kill you yet!"

Ki was on his back. He took a desperate gamble and used his left hand to grab a fistful of sand. He drove it up and into the man's eyes, blinding him. The mountain man fired his pistol blindly until he collapsed and died. Ki rolled sideways and came to his feet.

It was over.

The two mountain men had been worthy opponents, unusual men who had correctly anticipated the distance and speed of his swim and then been ready and waiting when he had dragged himself up on shore to build his small fire. Such men were always dangerous, and Ki considered himself fortunate to have vanquished them both.

Ki inspected his wound and determined that it was not especially serious. He ripped part of his shirt and bound the wound to stanch the bleeding. Then he turned his back on the two mountain men and headed into the forest. There was a road less than a hundred yards to his left that would take him to Scotty's Half Way House. Ki knew that if he hurried he could still be there by morning.

Jessie was worried and in a hurry as she and Griff Hastings disembarked from the Central Pacific Railroad at Dutch Flat and then set about supervising the loading of her four new cannons onto the huge freight wagons that she had telegraphed ahead to have waiting for them when they arrived.

"I still wonder if I shouldn't have bought six cannons," Jessie fretted.

Griff shook his head. "You said that the Yoders have only three side-wheelers. What do we need more cannons for?"

"In case you miss a couple of times."

"If I had six cannons instead of four, that would just mean we'd have to worry all the more. Besides, unless we're trapped, I have no intention of allowing our ship to take on three others all at the same time."

He patted Jessie on the shoulder. "Don't you worry. Four cannons are enough to do the job."

Billy Sawyer came rushing up from the rear passenger cars. "Our crew is all ready, Captain!"

"Good! No killings or stabbings on the way up from Sacramento?"

Billy shook his head. "No, sir! I told them what would happen if they fought either among themselves or with the other passengers. They've been on their best behavior, Captain."

Griff nodded with satisfaction. "Then load them up, three to each cannon. We will be departing within the hour."

Billy nodded. He looked excited. "Miss Starbuck, wait until those Yoder fellas see our men and those cannons. They're going to be in for a hell of a surprise, aren't they!"

"I hope so," Jessie said. The cannons were so heavy that they had to use oxen to pull the wagons, and that meant that it would be a long, slow ride. But there was no help for that. Jessie knew she could not take Griff and race ahead to find Ki and the *Tahoe*. The sailors needed a leader. They were rough and ready fighters, but they were men not accustomed to the mountains. They seemed a little cowed by the towering pine trees and the heavy forest.

Prospectors and freighters stared at them as if they were a curiosity—which they were, in their seaman's outfits and with their rolling walks.

It had not been easy getting good, tough seamen to leave the Barbary Coast. Jessie had been forced to pay exhorbitant wages, but she had not really minded. She had made it clear to each sailor who signed on with her that she expected trouble; after all, they weren't hauling four eight-pound cannons all the way up to Lake Tahoe for the fun of it.

"They're all ready," Griff said, taking a seat beside Jessie high up on the seat.

"Then let's get moving," Jessie said impatiently. She glanced sideways at the teamster beside her. "How long will it take to reach Scotty's Half Way House?"

"Two days. We ought to be there tomorrow evening if we don't break an axle or have any trouble."

Jessie swallowed her disappointment. On a fast horse she could reach Ki in less than five hours. It was going to be hard sitting here for two entire days, wondering if her samurai was alive and if he and Ken Bell had managed to get the *Tahoe* back into sailing condition. But most of all, Jessie wondered what in the world that conniving old devil, Clinton Yoder, was going to do next.

Clinton Yoder stood on what was left of his dock and surveyed the destruction. One ship completely destroyed, with its boiler and engine at the bottom of the lake, and his other two vessels badly damaged.

"Every damned one of you who saw that slant-eyed sonofabitch last night, step forward!"

The men were lined up at attention. Now at least thirty of them stepped forward.

Old Clinton's face turned scarlet, then purple with anger. "So every last damn one of you men admit to seeing the Chinaman and not being able to put a bullet through his damned brisket!"

He glared at them. "And because of your failure, I've lost a good ship and have two more badly damaged. Fortunately, I have the timber already cut to build new paddle-wheels. And we'll do it in record time."

"If we work all night," Arnie said hopefully, "I figure that we can get one of 'em fixed by—"

"Shut up, damn you!" Clinton raged. "We'll have a ship ready by tomorrow."

Arnie and Fred retreated into silence. Stung by their father's sharp words and ridicule, they seethed with humiliation. Both remembered the samurai with burning hatred.

Clinton Yoder glared at his sons, and then at his men. "Scotty and them son of a bitches that he hangs out with will be expecting us to attack today. They might even outnumber us, and I see no reason to play their game. So we're going to wait. Let them worry while we get these side-wheelers back in order. Come the day they're ready, we're going to steam on down this here lake. The first thing we'll do is blow the *Tahoe* right out of the water. And the second thing is going to give me even more pleasure. That's when we stand offshore and level Scotty's place. Just wipe it clean off the shore until it ain't nothing but a bunch of smokin' kindlin' wood."

The men smiled. Fred and Arnie lifted their heads. "What about the samurai?"

"He dies," Clinton said. "We wipe out Scotty's, and

156

then, when everything is burning, we come ashore and overrun the place. Anyone that puts up a fight is going to Boot Hill for their trouble. It's just that simple."

"And what about the woman?" Fred asked, remembering the swell of her fine breasts. "I sure would like to take her alive."

"Oh," Clinton said, "we'll do that all right. I got men waiting for her at the train stations both at Donner and Dutch Flat. When she comes back, they're to grab her and bring her here."

"You got it all planned, all right," Arnie said.

Clinton stared at the devastation. "You bastards are so dumb that it's a good thing that I still got brains above my pecker. Now get your asses to work on those boats. The sooner we get new paddle-wheels on 'em, the sooner we're going to have us some fun."

But the chance for "fun" came sooner than Clinton had expected. Two days later, a rider arrived on a heavily lathered horse, and was admitted directly into the rock fortress to see the old timber king.

"She came back and loaded four cannons at Dutch Flat," the rider said, not wasting any words.

Clinton pounded the table with fury. "Son of a bitch!" he screamed. "I should have guessed. But who's—"

The rider interrupted. "Mr. Yoder, along with the cannon is a crew of sailors. Rough looking men. Heavily armed."

Again the old man screeched with fury and outrage. "Sailors from the Barbary Coast! I should have guessed that much too! Should have known that Ken Bell didn't have the balls anymore to captain against me." Clinton glared at the man who had dared to bring him such bad tidings. "Where are they now?"

"They're still a little north of Sand Point. Won't be reaching Scotty's until this evening."

"How are they traveling?"

"Four wagons pulled by oxen, each one carrying a cannon and some sailors as guards."

"Where is the Starbuck woman?"

"First wagon, on the seat between two men."

Clinton turned and began to pace back and forth. "I want to hit them, and hit them with everything we've got," he said. "I want to drive those goddamn wagons and their guards and cannons right to the bottom of the lake."

"The Pritchard's Cut is the place to do it," the rider said. "But you're going to have to hurry."

Clinton nodded. Pritchard's Cut was *exactly* the right place to do it. It was a spot where the road lifted and cut in high over the water. There was a steep drop into the lake, and the water was very, very deep.

"You did well, Monty."

The rider nodded. "Want me to come along with you?"

Clinton nodded. "Yeah," he said. "Maybe you can keep my fool sons from getting their heads blown off."

"Those boys are good shots and hard fighters, Mr. Yoder. You don't need to worry a thing about them when the lead starts to flying."

Clinton was still angry about his boats, but he had to admit that the samurai's successful raid was not entirely the fault of either of his sons. And it was true, both his boys could sling lead with the best of them. Clinton always thought of Fred and Arnie as being quick on the trigger, but slow on the think.

The old man slammed one hand into the other. "We're going to get them today. Sink the cannon, wagons, and the whole works, and take the girl for pleasure and samurai-bait. It's even going to be better than I'd expected."

"I wouldn't miss it for anything," Monty said. "I heard that Miss Starbuck is as pretty as she is rich."

"Some men would say so," Clinton drawled. "If she'd been an ugly woman, my boys would have finished her and the samurai off the first time they laid eyes on them. As it was, they let their guard down and they paid for it. Hell, *I've* paid for it! But they won't make that same mistake again."

Monty nodded. "Boss," he said, "I think we better ride hard for Pritchard's Cut. If they get there first it ain't going to do us much good."

Clinton nodded. He grabbed his Winchester from the rifle rack and headed for the door. "You can get yourself a fresh horse from the stable, Monty. And while you're at it, saddle mine."

"Sure, boss," the rider said, "whatever you say."

The freighter shifted on his seat and began to crack his whip over the backs of the oxen. *"Yaaa!* Oxen *pull!"* he yelled over and over as the whip cracked loudly.

The freighter glanced sideways at Jessie. "You and Hastings better hang on tight, Miss Starbuck. This hill goes over Pritchard's Cut, and it's steep and dangerous. In the spring when it's muddy, or in the winter when there's ice on the road, a man sure earns his pay drivin' a team over this cut. Why, one mistake and you'd go tumbling down into that water far below and they'd never get you out."

As the big wagon rocked and swayed up Pritchard's Cut, Jessie gripped the seat hard. It was a steep hill, and the oxen were struggling to pull the huge wagon and her heavy cannon. The oxen bawled and their massive backs, corded with muscle, were knotted as they leaned into their traces and groaned with the effort.

Watching them struggle and scramble, Jessie felt guilty. "Griff," she said, "I think I'll lighten their load and get off right here to walk the rest of the way to the top."

The freighter frowned. "Your weight don't mean

nothin', and I can't stop on this uphill. They might not be able to get started again."

"Don't stop then," Jessie said. "I'll jump."

"Hell," Griff said, "I won't be made to look lazy. I'll walk along with you."

So they both hopped off the seat. It was a good six-foot drop to the side of the trail, but both landed without injury.

"You feel better about it now?" Griff asked as they hiked along beside the wagon.

"Some."

"I don't."

Jessie stopped a few hundred feet on and caught her breath. In this thin mountain air it was easy to find yourself out of breath very quickly. She moved to the edge of the road and waved up at the next freight wagon, letting him pass.

"Got to keep them moving, Miss Starbuck," the freighter shouted.

As the second wagon rolled slowly by, Jessie glanced at her cannon and saw how taut the thick ropes were that held it in place. The sailors in the back of the wagon were hanging on to those ropes and looked plenty nervous.

Jessie and Griff continued walking. "What do you think of the lake?" Jessie asked her new captain.

"Looks kind of small," he replied.

"Small! This is a huge lake."

"Not after sailing the seas, Jessie. Why, I could sail from one end of this to the other and hardly set my sails before it would be time to trim them and turn back around. She looks as calm as glass."

"Don't be fooled," Jessie said. "There's a strong wind that comes up in the afternoons."

"Yeah," he said, "I'll bet it's a regular gale that blows out there. Rollers as high as sixty, seventy foot tall, even."

Jessie frowned at him. Griff Hastings was a brave and

160

bold man and a great lover, but he could be a little sarcastic at times. He was not the easiest man in the world to be around when he got away from salt water.

"Sure be a hell of a drop," Griff said, peering over the side.

"Yes, it would be."

Right that minute they looked directly into each other's eyes. Each had the same flash of warning. But it was too late. From out of the trees just above Pritchard's Cut, a dozen rifles opened up. Even worse, men with pry bars began to send huge boulders crashing down into the wagons.

"Look out!" Jessie cried as a boulder swept past her and struck the third wagon. The wheel cracked and the wagon was knocked over the edge. Jessie heard sailors scream as the wagon and its team just vanished.

Jessie was wearing a gun, but she knew she and Griff were as good as dead if they tried to fight. There were just too many rifles firing too damned fast. She could see her other wagons being struck by thundering boulders. She saw a sailor manage to leap out, only to be cut down in a volley of rifle-fire. Griff was shooting, but she grabbed his arm and yelled, "Over the side!"

"You mean . . ."

A bullet plucked his hat off and sent it spinning out over the lake. They both jumped. The drop was probably eighty feet straight down. Jessie hung onto her six-gun and tried to prepare herself for impact with the lake.

But there was no way to prepare for the glimpse she caught of dying men, crashing wagons, flying cannon and thrashing, falling oxen. Everything crashed into the lake, and when Jessie hit the water the impact was like hitting a brick wall at a full gallop. She was momentarily dazed, and Griff caught her arm and pulled her toward the rocks.

161

"Those bastards are sniping on us from above!" Griff shouted. "Get under the rocks, Jessie!"

Jessie grabbed a rock and ducked under the line of fire. She knew she was hidden from the view of the riflemen, who had charged to the edge of the road and were now pouring a murderous fire down toward the shouting sailors and the teamsters.

"On, no!" she whispered, as a sailor grabbed his face and then disappeared in a swirl of crimson. "No!"

Some of her sailors had died at the moment of impact. Others had been caught in the lines of the oxen and had been drowned. A few had been thrown out from the falling wreckage and were desperately trying to swim straight out into the lake and beyond rifle range. They were all target practice, and not one of them was able to escape. But by shouting instructions, Jessie and Griff were able to get a few sailors to swim to the base of the cliff and take cover from the ambushers above.

It broke Jessie's heart to see the oxen all tangled up in the lines as they tried vainly to swim away. Some just gave up and drowned; a few broke free and swam to the rocks where the sailors pushed them away in the hope that they would swim either north or south and find a sandy beach. One, a big brindle, did exactly that and at least four followed it to safety.

A few were shot by the riflemen up above, though Jessie had no idea why unless it was simply to satisfy blood lust.

"We'll kill them all!" Griff vowed, hugging the rocks and cursing in helpless fury. "They got Billy!"

Jessie had forgotten about Billy Sawyer. In the midst of the chaos, she had simply not remembered him. But now his absence hit her very hard.

"Which wagon was he riding in?"

"The last one. He was worried about an attack from

162

behind." Griff pointed to a place where only a Stetson floated. "That's where it went in upside-down. He and the boys in it never had a chance."

Jessie swallowed the huge lump that had built in her throat. "I should have—"

"What?" he demanded. "What could you have done to prepare for this?"

Jessie had no answer. She had never even been along this awful stretch of dirt road known as Pritchard's Cut. But had she realized there was such a terribly dangerous place as this, she would have taken extra precautions.

"Look!" Griff shouted. "The son of a bitches only knocked three of them over. The first one, the one we were on, must have broken right in the road. But they've killed the driver and the men!"

It was true. The driver's body came dropping past them to strike the water with a great splash. Three more bodies came hurtling downward, arms swinging like rag dolls. Jessie recognized the men by their clothes as being the ones that had been riding in their wagon.

The bodies were followed by a booming voice that sounded like God's, the way it echoed across the water. "This lake belongs to me! Get out of this basin before I finish you all!"

Jessie clenched her fists and scrubbed at the tears that mixed with the cold, clear water. If it was the last thing she did on this earth she was going to see that Clinton Yoder, his sons, and their logging operation were destroyed so completely there would never even be a trace of their passing.

Jessie watched a floundering oxen finally give up trying to untangle itself. The poor beast just sank, and it pulled two more down with it.

This was war.

Griff shouted to the sailors who clung shivering to the

rocks. "Men, there's a cannon up above and we got to save it or this thing is over before it starts. So who's coming with me?"

"To where?" a sailor cried, craning his head up at the cliff that towered straight up to the road.

Griff scrubbed water from his eyes. "We'll flank the sons of a bitches. You, you, and you!" he said, pointing to the sailors. "You men move along the cliff to the south and get out as soon as you can. You still have guns?"

"Knives is all I got," one said.

"I got a gun, but it's all wet."

"Of course it's wet!" Griff shouted. "So's mine!"

"And mine," Jessie said. "But by the time we reach the road above, they'll be dry."

"She's right," Griff said. "And if they ain't gone yet, they'll sure wish they were! So let's get up there and get even, boys!"

The sailors nodded. There was murder in their eyes. One thing Jessie knew for sure. She and Griff had picked real fighters. Men who spat in the eye of long odds. Men who wanted to get even.

Chapter 15

Jessie would never forget what a cold and terrible job it was inching along the rocks until they could finally slip undetected into a tangle of manzanita and drag their shivering bodies out of the lake. Griff assumed the slow, painful task of cutting his way through the manzanita with his knife. By the time they reached the forest, Griff's arms were badly lacerated and his face was torn by those sharp, tough bushes.

Jessie crawled up beside him, wondering if the three sailors who had gone in the opposite direction had been able to get out of the lake yet. "I'm afraid I never expected it would start off like this," she said.

But the powerful seaman just grinned. "Hell, Jessie, I hated to lose good sailors, but they knew what they were up against. Even Billy did. You told us we were going to be badly outnumbered. We just got off to a bad start."

"The cannons are lost."

"Only *three* of the cannons are lost," he corrected. "There's still one up on top. If they were smart, they'd get all their men behind it and push it over the edge to join the others. But maybe they aren't so smart after all. If we can get it back and then use it against them, we can even the odds."

"Why haven't they destroyed it already?" Jessie asked.

"I don't know. That's what we've got to find out in a big hurry. So dry your weapons and let's go!"

Jessie was ready, and so were the two sailors right behind her. Altogether, they numbered only seven, but they would all fight to the death. She wished that Ki were here too, but if they could just save this cannon and get it mounted on the *Tahoe,* maybe they'd have a chance to do some damage of their own.

It was a long, hard scramble up the steep, rocky mountainside. Pritchard's Cut seemed almost impossible to reach, and Jessie knew that they would be helpless if the Yoder people spotted them from up above. But the Yoders hadn't bothered to see if there were any survivors, and when Jessie, Griff, and their two sailors finally struggled up to the edge of the road, there was no one waiting to gun them down.

"Check your weapons one more time," Griff said, nodding to a bend in the road just ahead. "When we go around that corner, we ought to run smack-dab into the bunch of them. Just up there is where we were attacked."

Jessie checked her gun. It was a .38-caliber Colt revolver, specially designed for its balance and lightness. She, Griff, and the other men were all wearing cartridge belts around their waists, but the ammunition in the belts was still too wet to use. However, Jessie was more than ready to face Yoder and his killers.

They moved swiftly up the dirt road, the very same road that she and Griff had hiked what now seemed like a lifetime ago. When they came to the hairpin corner that she remembered, Griff slipped in close to the cut in the rocks and raised his gun. "We take them fast and hard," he said. "If there's so many that we don't have a chance, then run to the cliff and dive back into the lake. We know how to get in close to the rocks in order to slip under their line of fire. Revenge is no good if we're all dead."

"I'm not going back over that cliff," a sailor growled. "Not unless it's my dead body they throw off the edge."

"I feel the same way," Jessie told him.

"Me too," the other sailor replied. "That's too damned far to jump, and the water is too cold. A second leap would kill me for certain."

"All right," Griff said, "then we fight to the finish. Let's go!"

They rushed around the corner and opened fire, catching the Yoder men by surprise. Jessie pulled her trigger as fast as she could take aim. Caught flat-footed with their guns holstered, five Yoder men were killed in the first volley, and the others jumped for their horses or panicked and bolted for cover. But the Yoders themselves were gone.

One of her fighting Barbary Coast sailors died with a grunt, but the other three, the ones who had gone in the opposite direction, suddenly appeared on the road. They caught the Yoder men in a withering crossfire. Griff and two sailors went dashing into the forest, chasing their fleeing enemies. Jessie heard gunshots, and she knew that more Yoder men were dying.

She had emptied her six-gun, so she reloaded using ammunition left by the fleeing Yoder men. But the battle was over. They had either routed or killed their enemies, though Jessie knew that it might well have been a different story if the Yoders themselves had remained instead of leaving just a dozen men behind.

At least now Jessie understood why the Yoders had not dragged or pushed the last cannon over the cliff. It was buried under what was left of an overturned freight wagon, which had caught fire. There had simply been no way that anyone could reach the cannon until the wagon had burnt down all around it and the ashes had cooled. Clinton Yoder had realized that, and had left these men to shove it over the cliff.

But where had the Yoders gone in such a hurry?

"Look what we caught!" Griff Hastings called as he and his men led a wounded ambusher out from the forest. "This one decided he'd rather make peace than take another bullet. Personally, I was hoping he'd change his mind."

Jessie was in a hurry. "Where did the Yoders go?" she demanded.

The man had taken a bullet through the heavy muscle of his upper arm. He was a rough looking fellow with rotting teeth and a white cast to one eye. Instead of answering Jessie, he just spat at her feet.

Griff's powerful hand shot out and he put a viselike grip on the man's wounded arm. Suddenly, the ambusher wasn't nearly so tough or insolent. He dropped to his knees as Griff's thumb punched into the bullet hole. His face, already pale, went positively ashen.

Jessie was shocked at Griff's ruthlessness, and yet she knew that lives depended on getting the truth out of this man in a big hurry.

"Stop!" the man begged. "You're killing me!"

Griff's face was savage with anger. "No," he growled, "you and your bloody friends killed *my* friends. Now answer the lady's question or I'll drive my thumb clear to the bone!"

No one who saw Griff's face could have doubted he'd carry out his threat. The ambusher sobbed and then cried, "All three of them went to attack the *Tahoe!*"

"Where is it?"

"Still at Hunter's Cove! They haven't gotten it off the beach yet!"

"Dear heavens," Jessie whispered. "If they catch that vessel in drydock, it's all over."

Griff twisted the man's bleeding arm behind his back and bent it high up between his shoulder blades. "Get on your feet!" he ordered.

The man had no choice but to jump to his feet. To have resisted would have meant that his arm would have been torn out of its socket. Jessie hadn't a clue as to what Griff was going to do next. When it happened, it was so fast that it took them all by surprise, especially their captive. One moment he was standing among them; the next moment he was being driven forward by Griff. He screamed. Then Griff hurled him off the cliff, and he went spinning down, end over end, and struck the lake below, sending a geyser of water into the air.

Jessie raced to the edge of Pritchard's Cut and stared down at the lake. The man disappeared under the surface in a pool of white, foaming bubbles. "Griff!" she cried in shock. "What if he drowns?"

Griff folded his arms across his chest and said nothing as he watched the surface of the water to see if the man would bob to the top. Seconds passed, then a minute, then a minute and a half, and still no sign of the wounded Yoder man.

"Hmmm," Griff mused aloud. "I would have bet anything the man could swim. He just *looked* like a swimmer to me. Guess I was wrong."

Griff turned away from the lake and stared at the smoldering remains of the wagon. "We've got to get that cannon out of there and to a safe place before those Yoders come back through here and kick it over the side. Jessie, about the only thing we can do is commandeer the first wagon that comes around the bend. Then we can only hope

169

that the cannon has cooled down, and that there's enough of us to lift it on board."

Jessie turned away from the water. The man had drowned. She figured that he deserved no better. None of the Yoder men that they'd shot had deserved any better. But there was something a little frightening about Griff Hastings. When he fought, he fought without any reservations, and there was no hesitation whatsoever in him if a killing was warranted in his mind. Tossing that wounded man over the cliff had proven that much. Jessie was just mighty glad that he was on her side. Teamed with Ki, the pair would seem almost indestructible.

Ki stood on the deck of the *Tahoe* and looked down into the shallow blue water. He turned to wave at Ken Bell and the men who had just pushed their stern-wheeler off the beach. The job had been almost finished when he had returned from his raid on the Yoder vessels, but Ki had been able to help with the last few yards. Getting the big stern-wheeler back down the rolling logs and into the cove had sure been a lot easier then jerking the vessel up and out of the water.

"Come on aboard!" he shouted to the sweating, exhausted men. "We'll steam on down to Scotty's Half Way House on a trial run."

The two dozen or so men who had helped seemed more than eager to wade out into the water and hop up on the deck. There was a mood of triumph and excitement as Ki threw more and more wood into the firebox and got the steam built up to a good head of pressure. He blasted the whistle several times, and Ken Bell was roundly cheered when he brought a couple of bottles of whiskey from some secret place in the wheelhouse. "Men," he announced, raising a bottle high over his head. "I've been saving this

170

stuff for just this occasion. You just mix it with a little Tahoe water and I guarantee you've got the finest drink ever known to man."

A man laughed. "What wrong with drinking it straight?"

"Suits me," Ken told them. He passed one of the bottles. But before it touched any man's lips, he said, "I want to drink a toast to Ki here, who fights like a wildcat and works harder than any man alive. I guess he's about the finest warrior I've ever known. And I also toast his boss, the beautiful Miss Jessica Starbuck, who bought this vessel and who could have gotten out of the deal after the Yoders shot the ass end off of her with cannon right here in Hunter's Cove not so very many weeks ago. But to her credit and my undying gratitude, Miss Starbuck never thought of backing out of our deal. And because of that, I got something to show for my life again besides a wooden leg."

"Aw shut up, Ken, and let's get this big son of a bitch turned around and headed down the shore to Scotty's! These two bottles aren't hardly enough to wet our lips."

Ken drank deeply and then hobbled up the ladder to the wheelhouse. He checked the steam gauge and signaled to Ki that the *Tahoe* had built up enough pressure and that he did not need to pitch any more wood to her fire.

Ki turned from the woodpile and felt the new paddle-wheel they had constructed slowly begin to churn at the lake. The water boiled up and the *Tahoe* began to back out of the cove.

Suddenly, Ki saw a movement, a flash of sunlight on metal. He spun around to see big Clinton Yoder, his two sons, and a large body of horsemen burst out of the trees on the run. The Yoder horses were heavily lathered, and it was clear they had raced hard to catch the *Tahoe* while she was still on shore. Clinton bellowed orders, and his small

171

army bailed off their horses, grabbing and firing their carbines.

The men aboard the *Tahoe* hit the decks. Ki heard the thump-thump of lead slugs striking the hull. On the upper deck, glass shattered as the newly replaced windows of the wheelhouse were blown out. But Ken and Ki had taken the precaution of building a protective wall of thick pine across the front and rear of the precious metal boiler. It was enough to stop a .30-.30 slug at long range, and that clearly infuriated Clinton Yoder and his sons. They cursed and hopped up and down on a beach that grew smaller and smaller as the boat pulled away.

Now a half-mile out on the lake, Ki, Ken, and the others were on their feet again, waving and jeering at the vanishing Yoders.

"You sure we want to go to Scotty's?" someone asked. "Don't you figure that's where *they're* goin' next?"

"Then that's all the more reason to steam down there and warn them," Ki said as he headed back to the woodpile and began to throw more fuel to the firebox.

The steam built higher and higher, and the huge paddle-wheel seemed to spin and drive their stern-wheeler ahead like a thing gone wild. Foam and white water churned up into the air and created a big rainbow. It would have been a pretty thing to watch if Ki was not so busy keeping the fires burning red hot.

He did not know if Clinton Yoder intended to try and wipe out Scotty or not. But if that was his plan, the samurai wanted to be where the fighting would take place. With luck, it would all be said and done and they would emerge victorious even before Jessie returned with her sea captain from San Francisco. And knowing Jessie, she would feel almost cheated.

• • •

Clinton Yoder was so goddamn mad he could have strangled his horse and then his two idiot sons. "I thought that vessel was supposed to be drydocked!" he screamed.

No one, especially his sons, said a word. Besides, it was obvious that they were only minutes late. If they had not had to wait at Pritchard's Cut for nearly two hours before the ambush of the freight wagons they could have caught the *Tahoe* on this beach and easily overrun Bell and his men and destroyed her. Burn her right to the sand and been finished with the threat of another logging vessel on this lake.

"At least we got the cannon, Pa," Arnie said, trying hard to console his father. "And as for that ship, as soon as we get ours back to working again, we can easily chase the *Tahoe* down, corner her, and send her to the bottom with our cannon."

Clint slammed his fist down on his saddlehorn and cursed loud and strong. "I don't know," he said finally. "Things just don't seem to be going the way they should."

"But Pa," Fred whined, "we wiped out those wagons at Pritchard's Cut and sent the cannon to the bottom of the lake. Them and all those sailors and teamsters. We just about the same as finished this so-called 'timber war' already."

"Have we?" Clinton remounted his horse.

"We gonna go wipe out Scotty and burn his place to the ground now?" Arnie asked hopefully.

Clinton thought about it for a minute. "There might be a lot of men at Scotty's, teamsters and such, that are pretty fair rifle shots."

"We're not afraid to take 'em, Pa," Arnie said, puffing out his chest.

Clinton looked at his son with pure disgust. "If we wait

173

until we can sail, we can bring our side-wheelers down here, stand off from Scotty's, and blow it apart with our cannon without risking a single life. That's the way a smart man chooses to do it."

Fred and Arnie flushed with anger and turned their horses away. They had wanted more blood and were disappointed. Seeing those freight wagons being bowled over like pins and then rolling off Pritchard's Cut and tumbling into the lake with men and animals all broken and drowning had been fun. They'd shot a few oxen, too.

It had been a damn good day's work until they'd arrived to see the *Tahoe* steaming away just out of rifle range. But hell, it was going to be pretty special to see Scotty's Half Way House go up in smoke and fire. See little figures scurrying around helplessly on the shore as their own cannon did its deadly work.

Yeah, that would really be something. And so would be chasing down the *Tahoe* and blowing her all to hell.

Chapter 16

When Ki first saw the cliff below Pritchard's Cut and the floating debris, he felt a chill sweep through his lean body. But then his eyes lifted to the cut itself. Even though the distance was great, he could still recognize that a small group of men were trying to lift something very, very heavy into the bed of a wagon. There was a thin cloud of smoke drifting up toward the sky.

"Here," Ki said, stepping aside from the firebox so that others could take his place. He took the ladder steps two at a time. When he reached the wheelhouse, Ken Bell was already starting to guide the *Tahoe* in toward shore. He blasted his steam whistle again and again, and the people on Pritchard's Cut stopped their exertions. After a moment they began to wave.

"It's Miss Starbuck," Ki said, recognizing her copper-colored hair. "Full speed ahead!"

"If I did that, I'd run her right up onto the beach. I wouldn't guess Miss Starbuck would be too pleased to see us wreck her ship again."

Ki could not argue with that, although he was more than impatient to be rejoined with Jessie. Ki had a million questions to ask her, and yet he would ask nothing. He realized full well that she would tell him everything that was important and worth knowing.

"That looks like a good place to beach, just to the south of the cliff," Ed decided aloud.

The *Tahoe* steamed in toward shore. When Ki was finally able to jump onto the sand, Jessie was waiting for him. She wasted no time in explaining the tragedy that had befallen her sailors, the freighters, and their wagons. "We've got one cannon up on the road. If we can get it aboard the *Tahoe,* then we've got a fighting chance, Ki."

"What about cannonballs and powder?"

"There are cannonballs spilled all over the road. As for powder, well, we just have to hope that Scotty can provide us with a barrel."

Ki nodded. He saw the powerful figure of a seaman standing up on the road. "Is he your man?"

"No," Jessie said. "You are my man. But Griff Hastings is a fighter and a sea captain. He'll stand up against Yoder's three ships, and I think he's got a fighting chance of beating them at their own game."

Ki decided that they were in too much of a hurry to go into the details of how he had already incapacitated two Yoder ships and completely demolished the third. Besides, the Yoders might show up at any time, and the sooner they placed that cannon on the deck of this ship, the easier they'd all breathe.

"Hang on!" Ken Bell shouted from his battle-post on the second deck as the *Tahoe* nudged firmly against the sandy beach.

Ki, Jessie, and the men aboard the *Tahoe* all grabbed ropes and set off climbing up to Pritchard's Cut. It was a steep climb, though not a particularly long one. It took them less than an hour to reach Griff Hastings and his men.

Griff studied the samurai. "So," he said, extending his hand, "I've heard a lot about you."

Ki simply nodded. "We've come for the cannon."

176

Griff looked down at the *Tahoe*. "I can see all the way from here that you and your men have done an excellent job on the deck and paddle. So let's get this cannon on deck and bolted down securely, then let's sail on to victory."

"Today?" Jessie asked.

Griff squinted up toward the sun. "Tomorrow. Tell me this. Will the morning or evening sun blind our enemy?"

"The morning sun," Ki said.

"Good!" Griff rubbed his hands together with anticipation. "I've always preferred to attack at first light."

Ki nodded. Even though there were only two Yoder ships, and neither of them were operational for the time being, he knew that their cannon could still be turned and fired with great effectiveness if the Yoders had enough warning.

Without further discussion, they set about tying ropes to the cannon, which was still quite hot. They needed horses, mules, or oxen. But there were none available, so they threw their shoulders to the ropes and dragged that damned cannon almost two miles back down Pritchard's Cut until they came to the beach where the *Tahoe* was waiting.

Pulling the stubby cannon through the sand was impossible; it just sank. So they tied the ropes end-to-end and fastened them to a stanchion aboard the steamer. Then they backed the *Tahoe* out into the lake until the cannon was right at the water's edge. Then the paddles were reversed and the vessel returned to shore. Ken Bell did such a fine job that the bow of the *Tahoe* was brought to rest within five feet of the cannon.

"All right, men!" Griff shouted. "As many of the strongest among you as can get ahold of this damn thing, take a grip. Let's see if we can lift her!"

The strongest men crowded around. They gripped the hot iron and tried to lift the cannon, but it was too heavy.

"Ropes, then!" Griff shouted. "Take the ropes up on

deck. When we lift, everyone on board pull on those ropes! Ready now. One. Two. Three!"

This time the cannon plopped out of the wet sand. With a roar of effort, they were able to lift the heavy piece of artillery and ease it onto the deck. The *Tahoe* almost immediately settled deep in the sand.

"Christ!" Griff said. "With all this weight on the bow, we might have beached her."

But Ken Bell reversed the paddles once more and the engine whined powerfully as its huge paddles churned hard to pull the *Tahoe* off the beach. When the vessel broke free, a shout of triumph erupted from the men. They made one quick trip back up to Pritchard's Cut to collect cannonballs, and then everyone waded out and climbed on board.

Jessie hugged her samurai. "I knew you would have this ship ready!"

"I had a lot of help," Ki said. "And what about you in San Francisco?"

"I'll tell you about that on the way back to the Comstock. Right now, all I can think about is getting this stern-wheeler to Scotty's, getting some powder, and then having Griff and his sailors take command of this ship for tomorrow's attack."

Ki decided he had better tell Jessie about his own attack on the Yoder vessels and pier, and so he called Griff aside. When he was finished Jessie could not believe the wonderful news, but Griff seemed strangely subdued. "Hell," he growled, "with their ships out of order, it sure doesn't shape up to be much of a battle. Especially if we catch them asleep."

"Maybe we won't," Jessie said.

As the *Tahoe* steamed south, Griff almost looked as if he hoped not.

⚫ ⚫ ⚫

They had now taken on powder, and despite the fact that Ki and Griff had begged Jessie to remain at Scotty's, she would have none of it. "I own this ship, and I'll be danged if I'll sit here and worry!"

"She always this stubborn?" Griff asked.

"Yes," the samurai replied.

They said goodbye to Ken Bell and his small family, then sailed north under a full head of steam long before daybreak. The air had a nip to it, and even though they all knew that the Yoder ships were not expected to be able to confront them, they were still on edge.

"They'll hear our paddles and engine at least five miles before we get within cannon range," Griff predicted. "Sound carries too well across water, and there is no way we can drive this vessel into their cove without letting them know far in advance."

Jessie and the sailors were armed with Winchester rifles. Scotty and a few volunteers had also come aboard to help fight. They had more than twenty cannonballs. They meant to end the reign of the ruthless Yoder family once and for all.

Dawn found them three miles from the rock fortress. Captain Griff Hastings had the throttle open wide, and the *Tahoe* was shaking as it plowed forward at maximum speed. Griff had ordered their lone cannon bolted to the front deck of his vessel. Three experienced men were ready to handle the barrage.

But suddenly, out of the faint morning light, one of the Yoders' side-wheelers rounded the peninsula and came steaming straight for them.

Griff smiled. "Well, samurai, I guess it just goes to prove that if you own a sawmill and have the timber for paddles already cut you can rebuild a side-wheel steamer in a mighty big hurry."

Griff leaned out the empty window of his wheelhouse and called down to the three cannoneers. "You boys hold your fire until I blast my whistle. Then, let fly!"

"Aye, aye, sir!" came the reply.

Jessie stood frozen between her samurai and her captain. The distance between the boats closed, and when they were within a half-mile of the stern-wheeler, it suddenly swung to the right in order to put its cannon in a good firing position.

But Griff also swung hard to starboard and the *Tahoe* churned right at the Yoder ship. "Steady," Griff said to no one in particular. "Steady."

Suddenly he grabbed the whistle cord and yanked it hard. The mighty blast sounded, and just a moment later their cannon belched smoke and fire. Jessie saw a ball appear like a black dot drawn against the blackboard of sky. The ball seemed to float out toward the Yoder ship, then arc directly over its bow and hit the water.

"We missed!" she cried.

"Of course we did," Griff said without the slightest bit of disappointment or anger. "Those boys have never fired that particular cannon before. They need a practice shot or two to see how she goes."

Ki said, "Well, they had better learn pretty fast, because here she comes again."

Clinton Yoder had cut power, then reversed his engines. Great torrents of water were being flung toward an early morning sky. Their two portside cannons were now lined up on the *Tahoe,* and they fired simultaneously. Jessie clenched her hands together and held her breath even as Griff also cut power and reversed his paddle-wheel. The maneuver practically threw them to the floor.

The cannonballs sailed just across the bow of the *Tahoe,*

missing by less than twenty feet. Griff blasted his steam whistle again, and their lone cannon fired. This time they were on target, and their cannonball exploded through the side-wheeler's deck, setting it on fire immediately. Jessie saw men racing for buckets as Griff again reversed power and went right at the wounded ship.

"I don't want them all slaughtered if it can be helped," she told Griff in a firm voice.

"We have to send that ship to the bottom," he replied tersely, giving the *Tahoe* full power ahead.

Jessie waited as her heart filled with dread. Griff was closing the distance very quickly now, and when he was within two hundred yards, she knew that they could not miss. The Yoder vessel was badly hit. It listed to starboard. She could see Clinton Yoder in the wheelhouse with his two sons. Old Clinton was frantically attempting to turn the stern-wheeler, but she wasn't responding properly.

Griff yanked on the whistle cord again. Held it tight, and the *Tahoe* wailed like an avenging banshee as it steamed ahead. Again their cannon belched smoke and flame, and when their vessel pushed through its own smoke, Jessie was shaken to see that the entire wheelhouse was gone, along with the three Yoder men.

"No more, Griff," she told him. "We've won."

"No," he said through clenched teeth. "They slaughtered Billy and my sailors. I won't rest until every damn one of them is dead!"

The Yoder men were bailing out into the lake. The ship was now taking on water fast. Huge clouds of steam were rolling off the decks and men were being scalded alive.

"Enough!" Jessie yelled.

But Griff was not finished. In his world, no quarter was asked and none had ever been given.

Jessie yelled, "Ki, stop him!"

The samurai drove a punishing *tegatana* blow that caught Griff on the side of the face and should have dropped him. But the captain only staggered. He lunged for Ki and caught him by the shirtfront, then hurled him against the bulkhead so hard that Ki was dazed.

Griff went for Ki, and it was all the samurai could do to duck and avoid having his face rearranged. Ki wobbled backward and Griff hit him with a right uppercut that almost decapitated the martial-arts master.

Jessie drew her gun, but Ki saw the move and yelled, "No!"

Jessie holstered her gun and grabbed the steam throttle. There were Yoder men in the water up ahead, and they would be ground under her paddles if she didn't stop this ship and rescue them.

Griff came at Ki again, and the samurai feigned grogginess. Griff threw a punch, certain it would finish the fight. But Ki ducked and unleashed a flat-foot strike that connected with Griff's stomach. The seaman gasped and tottered backward. Ki used a sweep-kick to take the heavier, more powerful man's legs out from under him. But Griff did manage to grab Ki's pants leg and pull him down. The two rolled and fought as Jessie turned the wheel hard to avoid ramming the Yoder vessel.

When she turned around, both men were climbing to their feet. It was the samurai who unleashed a tremendous kick to Griff's face. A kick that actually lifted the seaman up and sent him through the doorway to topple down the ladder to the first deck, where he lay unable to move.

"Are you all right?" Jessie asked. Ki looked to be in pain but he was the one still standing.

"I'll live."

"Good. What do you suppose got into him? Is he a killer?" Jessie asked.

Ki shuffled over to the ladder and stared down at the prostrate captain. "He has never been beaten, and he does not understand mercy. Maybe from now on he will understand better."

Jessie hoped the samurai was correct. "Tell the men that there will be no slaughter. The Yoders are dead. Any of their men who fight will be left out here on the lake to swim or drown. I don't care. The others will be taken to shore and made to leave the Tahoe Basin."

Ki nodded with approval as Jessie brought the *Tahoe* around the peninsula of land and within sight of the rock fortress, the pier, and the last of the Yoder ships and the Yoder sawmill.

"What about them?" the samurai asked.

Jessie did not hesitate. She remembered too well how the Yoders had ambushed her men at Pritchard's Cut and had slaughtered them from the cliff above the water. "I want it all destroyed," she said. "Why don't you tell that to Captain Hastings when you get him revived."

"Good," he said. "I am glad you forgave what overcame him. All warriors cannot have the discipline of a true samurai. He is young, and he will learn."

Jessie smiled. "I know that. Maybe . . . maybe he finally needed a whipping to teach him a little humility. Humility is good for all of us, Ki."

"I know that too," the samurai told her. "But it is not easy to be humble sometimes."

Jessie glanced sideways at her dear friend. Even though he was straight-faced, she knew that he was making a joke of himself. "Ki," she said, "you are one in a million."

"I know," he replied, and then he hurried below and she heard his muffled laughter.

They had destroyed everything owned by Clinton Yoder and his sons. Griff had used his single cannon until the rock fortress had broken and crumbled like a house of cards. The sawmill had required only three cannonballs before it was consumed by flames. The last ship had been sunk and the pier blown to bits.

Now, as Jessie watched men pile her heavy timbering aboard the V and T Railroad to be taken up to the Comstock Lode, she knew that the arrival of strong shoring to the mines would be a godsend.

"Griff believes we can deliver a hundred thousand board-feet before winter," Jessie said. "I want Lil and Bert to share it with my own mine. We'll sell it to them on credit."

Ki said, "They also need some new machinery down in the mine itself and—"

"Why don't you take Lil down in the shaft and write a list of what's needed. How would you like that?"

Ki blushed and Jessie smiled devilishly, because neither of them had forgotten what Ki and Lil had done the last time they were underground.

"What about you?"

"I have a new mine, and it's going to take a little time to get the required timbering down into the Montezuma and get it back to full and safe production. Then too, Griff will need my attentions. We'll be starting our new sawmill right away."

Ki understood. Griff had become a better man since his whipping. He'd become more tolerant, less ruthless; though he still drove his sailors hard and demanding. Jessie enjoyed Griff, just as Ki would soon enjoy Lil Butler down in the Lucky Lady Mine.

Ki could hardly wait to see that girl once again.

184

Watch for

LONE STAR IN THE BIG THICKET

seventy-fourth novel in the exciting
LONE STAR
series from Jove

Coming in October!